THE
POISON ARROW
TREE

THE
POISON ARROW
TREE

SHEL ARENSEN

Kregel
Publications

The Poison Arrow Tree

© 2003 by Shel Arensen

Published by Kregel Publications, a division of Kregel, Inc., P.O. Box 2607, Grand Rapids, MI 49501.

Cover illustration: David Du

ISBN 0-8254-2041-5

Printed in the United States of America

03 04 05 06 07 / 5 4 3 2 1

To my delightful daughter, Malindi,
and the girls' gang at Acacia Academy in Naivasha.
May their years of growing up in Africa be as enjoyable as mine.

CHAPTER ONE

THE GENET CAT TRAP

"**O**uch! I hit a stinging nettle!" My leg burned. Jon and Matt, leading the way through the narrow, leaf-covered path, turned and gave me a withering look.

"Pipe down, will you, Dean?" Matt commanded, his messy blond hair framing his freckled face. "You'll scare every animal and bird in the woods."

I silently licked my hand and rubbed my saliva-slick palm over the nettle sting. Soon I would have an angry red welt on my thigh.

As captain of the Rugendo Rhinos, Matt Chadwick gave the orders in our club. Rugendo was the name of the mission station where we lived in the thickly forested highlands of Kenya. We called ourselves the Rhinos because that year Matt's dad had taken the four of us in our club to watch a special off-road race called the Rhino Charge, which raises money to help save rhinos from extinction. The drivers and their teams each received a map showing ten checkpoints. We watched the drivers and their off-road vehicles from the eighth checkpoint as they charged through the rocky bush. Since they could follow any route they wanted, each rig came in from a different direction. Matt cheered when an old jeep appeared out of a canyon. The first team to reach all ten checkpoints and get back to the start won.

So when we formed our club we decided to call ourselves the Rugendo Rhinos. We didn't have four-wheel-drive cars, but whether we hiked or rode our bikes, we loved bush-barging. And we let Matt direct us since we'd elected him club captain. He liked to be in front like his dad, who taught at a Bible school at Rugendo and held pastors' seminars around the country.

Jon Freedman motioned for us to follow. Crouching over with his air rifle held easily in his hand, he set off. Jon had only recently come to Kenya, but he could track animals through the forest and drill the bull's-eye when we had target practice with our air rifles. He loved to gut the pigeons we shot. Maybe he got his skill with a knife from his dad, a surgeon and the only doctor at our mission hospital.

Matt recognized Jon's skills and let Jon lead the way on our hikes through the forest. This Saturday we had said good-bye to books for the weekend and were looking for a good place to set our new genet cat trap.

Dave Krenden, the third member of our club, nudged me from behind with the wooden box he held in his arms. A ray of sunlight filtered through the trees and glinted off Dave's glasses that tilted slightly to the right. "Let's go," he whispered.

Dave had built the box himself. It was shaped like a long shoe box and had a sturdy wooden frame with heavy-duty mesh-wire screen stretched and stapled around it. He took after his dad who worked as a missionary builder. In fact, Dave had designed and almost single-handedly built our tree fort in the huge wild fig tree. We'd all helped, but Dave's building ability had finished the project.

The box Dave held now was our trap. If we could catch a genet cat, we would tan the skin for the wall of our fort.

I motioned for Dave to go ahead of me, massaged my leg a few more times, and followed. My name is Dean Sandler. My dad is a writer who edits a Christian youth magazine at Rugendo and trains Kenyan writers. I'd been elected our Rhino club secretary because the others figured if my dad could write, I could too. I really couldn't, but I managed to scribble enough to keep our club organized. We Rhinos always did everything together even though Matt was in sixth grade, I was in fifth, and Dave and Jon were in fourth.

Jon signaled for us to stop, and he knelt down behind a low bush. We huddled next to him. He pointed silently with his chin the way an African would. Pointing with a finger was not only rude in Africa, in this case the movement might have frightened the beautiful bushbuck at the bottom of the ravine. The wind shifted and a gust blew from behind us carrying our scent to the buck. He tensed, gave a sharp doglike bark, and bounded away into the forest.

"Beautiful," murmured Matt, "but let's find a hiding place to set our trap."

Jon said, "Come on. I know a good place under those big trees at the bottom of the ravine." We slipped down the steep bank until we hit the bottom where a small stream trickled during the rainy season. Now, at the height of dry season, the ravine bottom carried no hint of water. No rain had fallen for three months.

Jon got low to the ground and began casting about for tracks. Soon he found some small caves on the steep banks above the streambed. Jon peered in and picked up the digested shell-like rings of a millipede, a small wormlike creature. "Some genet cat has been here eating millipedes," he announced. "At the coast millipedes grow as big as hot dogs, but up here in the high country they stay pretty small."

"When my little brother, Craig, was three we went to the coast on vacation," I said. "He saw one of those millipedes crawling by, picked it up, and took a big bite. First we knew about it, he was screaming. Whatever's in a millipede's guts burned his mouth and his lips pretty bad."

"Your brother munched a giant millipede?" Matt made a face. "What did he think he was? A genet cat?"

Pointing at a nearby cedar tree, Jon said, "I think if we put the trap near the base of that tree we can catch ourselves a genet cat. The tracks show at least one genet comes by here looking for millipedes. He can't live too far away. So if we set our trap right and bait it well, maybe the genet cat will stop in for a pre-millipede meal."

Dave took the trap from under his arm. He laid it tenderly near the tree, like a mother setting her baby down for a nap. Sliding the door gently up and down, he made sure it would fall correctly. He tested the wire and nail he had devised as the spring mechanism. The nail went through a metal curtain ring on top of the door and the wire led from the nail over a small pulley to a bait stick at the far end of the box. If the bait stick was pulled, it jerked the nail out of the solid-wood door, which fell over the entrance trapping the genet cat. The trap worked perfectly, as Dave's creations always did.

"Now all we have left to do is to put some bait on the stick," Matt said, pulling a mostly empty jar of rancid peanut butter from his coat pocket.

"Gross!" I said. "The oil leaked all over your coat!"

Matt looked disgustedly at his oil-soaked coat and shrugged. "I guess it's my hunting coat from now on." Dipping his finger into the peanut butter, he dug out a large smear. He reached into the trap and plastered the bait stick with peanut butter. Dave set the trap carefully while Jon and I gathered leaves and dirt. We covered the trap inside and out to make it look as natural as possible.

Satisfied with our work, we stepped back. Jon broke a small branch from a tree and whisked away our footprints. We eased into the forest, arguing about who should check the trap and how often. After several minutes of bickering, Matt told us to be quiet. He gave us the order in which we would check the trap. He, of course, would be first and would check the trap early the next morning before church.

"Let's go by the pond below the hospital on our way back to Rugendo," I said. "Craig started first grade this year, and he wants a jarful of tadpoles for show-and-tell."

"Sure," Matt said. "You can even use my peanut butter jar. If you carry it, of course." He tossed the greasy jar to me. I caught it and held it an arm's length away from my clothes.

As we got near the pond we heard goats bleating and tearing at tree leaves. "I wonder who's watching these goats?" asked Dave.

"Looks like a fire over there," Jon said, pointing at some smoke curling into the air from behind a beautiful bushy tree with red berries growing on it.

As we came around the tree, we couldn't believe what we saw!

CHAPTER TWO

AN UNEXPECTED
DISCOVERY!

Two young Kenyan boys lay crumpled on the ground near a smoldering campfire.

"*Jambo! Habari?*" Matt said in greeting, asking how the boys were. They didn't respond. One of the boys twitched and a low hissing moan eased out of his lips.

"Maybe they're sleeping," I said timidly, not wanting to believe the worst.

"I don't think so." Jon edged closer. "Hey, wake up!" he said loudly.

Silence answered him. We could hear our own breathing. Dave and I stood rooted to the ground, but Matt and Jon reached down and tried to turn the boys over. The same boy who had earlier moaned now drew in a ragged breath of air.

"That's Kamau," Dave said when he saw the boy's face. "His dad is a carpentry *fundi*. He works with my dad on buildings for the churches and schools."

"Run get some help from the hospital," Matt commanded, looking at Dave and me. "It looks like Kamau is at least breathing, but

I think the other boy is finished. Hurry. Jon and I will stay here, but I really don't know what we can do."

"Pray," Jon suggested. That surprised me. He was usually so busy running through the forest hunting and trapping he didn't think too much about asking God for help, but this situation was beyond all of us.

"We'll pray as we run," I said, turning and sprinting up the path to the mission hospital. Dave ran close behind me until I bashed through a springy branch that had grown over the path. Forgetting to be polite and hold the branch back so it wouldn't slap Dave, I ran straight through it.

"Ouch!" Dave screamed behind me. I turned to see him bent on one knee with his hand over his eyes.

I stopped and turned back. "Are you all right?" I asked after my sides stopped heaving.

"I think so," Dave answered, "but that branch hit me smack in the face and whipped my glasses off. And my forehead stings."

I examined his face. The branch had left a nasty welt and some scratches above his eyebrows. "You've got a bit of a scratch," I said, "but your eyes seem to be OK."

"Except that I can't see without my glasses. Not even enough to find them." He was on his knees scrabbling his fingers through the stiff yellow grass.

I got down and found his glasses for him. Placing them back on, he remembered our mission and said, "Let's hurry to the hospital. I'll lead the way from here."

Arriving a few minutes later we ran up to Pastor Waweru, the hospital chaplain. "Where's Dr. Freedman?" Dave asked. "We need to see him right away!"

Pastor Waweru looked surprised. "What's wrong, boys?" he asked. "Dr. Freedman is in surgery, but perhaps I can help. Is one of you hurt?" He looked closely at the red mark on Dave's forehead.

"No, but two boys are sick, maybe even dead!" I blurted. "We need Dr. Freedman right away. Can't you please get him?"

"Let's go to the operating theater," Pastor Waweru said, walking us quickly down the corridor with a red concrete floor that reeked of antiseptic. "You can tell me what you mean as we walk."

"We saw two boys lying on the grass down by the pond," Dave said. "They look sick. One seems to be breathing a little. The other, well, we didn't see him move at all and . . ."

"We think he's dead," I finished. "And the other boy may be too if we don't get some help soon."

We had arrived at the operating theater and Pastor Waweru sent a nurse in to call Dr. Freedman.

"Do you know who these boys are?" Pastor Waweru asked, turning back to us.

Dave nodded. "The boy who's barely breathing is Kamau, the son of the carpenter who works with my dad, but I don't know the other . . ."

Pastor Waweru's face turned charcoal gray. "Kamau is my wife's nephew. He usually herds the goats with Ngugi who is my brother's wife's youngest brother."

Dr. Freedman stepped out of the operating room with a smile on his face. He slipped his mask down. "We saved both the baby and his mom," he said, pleased with his work. "What can I do for you boys?"

Pastor Waweru took him by the hand and pleaded, "Come quick. Two of my young relatives are sick, maybe even dead."

"We found them down by the pond," I put in. "Matt and Jon are there right now. Hurry! The boys need help real bad."

Dr. Freedman grabbed his medical bag and began to run, white coat flying out behind him. We had to sprint to catch up. Pastor Waweru called several Kenyan nurses to join us as we ran out of the hospital compound and down the path leading to the pond.

It was about half a mile to where we'd left Matt and Jon watching over Kamau and his fellow herdboy. Dr. Freedman and Pastor Waweru knelt over the two boys. Dr. Freedman put his head on Kamau's chest. "He's alive, but just barely," he said grimly, more to himself than anyone else. He turned to the other boy.

Pastor Waweru recognized the second boy's faced and cried out in dismay, "It's Ngugi."

Dr. Freedman felt for Ngugi's pulse and then listened to Ngugi's chest with his stethoscope. Looking up, he shook his head. "I'm sorry," he announced to those of us who had gathered. "This boy is dead." Without waiting for the finality of his words to hit us, he turned back to Kamau and said, "And this boy will be dead soon if we don't get him to the hospital." He bent down and picked up Kamau in his arms. Pastor Waweru stepped up to help him.

"Bring the other boy, too," Dr. Freedman called over his shoulder as they hustled up the path. I looked at Matt. His face looked as green as my stomach felt. The two Kenyan nurses stepped in front of us and picked up the limp body of Ngugi and carried him gently to the hospital.

We followed, not sure what else to do. At the hospital we sat in the outpatient lounge on white enamel-painted benches waiting to hear whether Kamau lived or died. Jon scuffed his feet back and forth on the mud-stained floor. He always had a hard time sitting still and waiting around was agony for him. Finally he stood up. "I'm going to find out what's going on from my dad." He marched into the main part of the hospital.

"Do you think he should go?" I asked, concerned that he (meaning *we*) might get in trouble.

Matt shrugged. "His dad runs the hospital. He can't get in too much trouble. Besides, I'm getting antsy sitting here myself. Do you have any idea what happened to those two boys? Jon and I looked closely to see if they'd been shot or something but couldn't see any blood or wounds or anything."

Jon returned with his dad. Dr. Freedman looked serious. "Thanks to your quick thinking and getting help, Kamau is alive, but only just. I'd like you boys to pray for him."

"What's wrong with him?" Matt asked.

"It puzzles me," said Dr. Freedman. "I have no idea what the sickness is or what caused it. Pastor Waweru says both boys were in fine health this morning when they went out to herd the goats. It's a mystery to me. We're going to try to do an autopsy on the boy that died. Maybe that will give us some clue to the cause. Right now we're doing everything we can to keep Kamau alive. There's not much more you boys can do. You might as well run along home."

Pastor Waweru came over and suggested, "Let's pray for Kamau and for the families of both boys." So, standing in a circle, we prayed and asked God to help Kamau to recover.

As we started to leave, a large group of Kenyans pushed through the door in a swarm. Some of the ladies wailed with loud, penetrating sobs.

"*Woooi, woooi,*" they cried in the haunting Kikuyu expression of grief. Tears streamed from their faces as they pushed toward Dr. Freedman and Pastor Waweru.

The crowd demanded to know what had happened to the two herdboys. Pastor Waweru gently explained that Ngugi had died and Kamau was alive but very sick. This news was greeted with more wails and tears. We Rhinos pushed ourselves against the shiny pink painted wall. My head pounded and my stomach churned. I wiped my sweaty palms on my shorts before shoving them into my pockets.

Now the crowd turned to Dr. Freedman and an older man, a fringe of white hair circling his bald head, asked, "What sickness caused Ngugi's death?"

"I don't know," Dr. Freedman admitted. The crowd quieted down. The women, all wearing brightly colored flower pattern headscarves, continued to sob and cry.

Pastor Waweru spoke up. "I know this is sad news for all of us. Even I am related to these two boys. Right now Kamau is barely alive. Ngugi is dead. I suggest we come before the Lord in prayer."

Most of the group nodded and Pastor Waweru began to pray. "Dear Lord, we come to you with sad hearts today. We don't understand what has happened, but we pray—"

"I know what happened!" a deep voice interrupted the prayer.

Everyone in the room turned. A large Kenyan man stood in the doorway, his eyes wide and bloodshot. The buttons on his worn white shirt threatened to break loose as his bulging stomach heaved in and out with his rasping breath. His jaw twitched and beads of sweat dripped off his face. He took a step closer and glared at everyone.

"My son Ngugi is dead, and I know who is responsible," he

said. He took a deep breath to emphasize his next statement. "Baba Kamau, you put a curse on my son!"

Baba Kamau, Kamau's father, looked shocked. "Put a curse on your son? I would never do that. What do you mean? My son is sick, too, and at the point of death. How can you accuse me?"

"You were jealous of my son's success in school," Ngugi's father said. "I know that Kamau's school results were not as good as Ngugi's. You knew that Ngugi would go on to university and help my family out of our poverty. You couldn't stand to see us get ahead. So you went to a witch doctor and cursed my son. Now he's dead."

"I did not," Baba Kamau protested, but Ngugi's father acted as deaf as if he had stuffed two maize cobs in his ears.

"You are going to pay," Ngugi's father shouted, eyes rolling in rage. "I will get my revenge. I believe you cursed my son. I will go to the witch doctor to confirm this, and I will put an even more powerful curse on you and your whole family! Listen, everyone, and remember my words. Calamity will strike the home of Baba Kamau. I have said it!"

Ngugi's father turned and strode out of the hospital. Everyone, including us Rhinos, stood stunned. We had no idea what would happen next.

CHAPTER THREE

THE SHADOW BY THE POND

The crowd of people began to murmur, filling the room with the low gurgling sound of many voices. One wide-hipped woman fainted to the ground, her full, multiflowered skirt fluttering down like leaves swirling in the wind. Pastor Waweru moved quickly to help. Jon's dad shook his head from side to side. He looked confused. He turned and looked at us backed up against the wall. Frowning, he said, "You boys should get on home. Try to forget what you saw and heard here. The people will get over it. They're all just emotional about Ngugi's death. They'll go home, plan the funeral, and it'll all be over. Just get home. You did well to save Kamau's life. Let's pray he doesn't die as well."

Pastor Waweru came over to Jon's dad and, taking him by the arm, led him aside. He began to speak rapidly and earnestly, eyes widening as he talked.

Matt nudged me. "Let's get out of here," he whispered. We crept quietly to the heavy wood and glass doors, pushed them open, and escaped into the sunshine. I looked down at the greasy peanut butter jar I still grasped in my hand. I said, "We'd better go back to the pond. I never got the tadpoles for Craig."

"Not me," said Matt. "Going back there will remind me of what Kamau and Ngugi looked like lying on the ground. I want to forget it. I'm going home to see if my mom made any cookies." With that he jogged off.

"I have to go home, too," Jon said and left abruptly.

I looked at Dave. "Wow, they're scared, aren't they?" Dave said.

"I'd probably be scared, too, if I'd stayed by the dead boy like they did." I paused. "Do you want to go with me?"

"Why not?" Dave shrugged.

Arriving back at the pond I wiped the peanut oil on my hands off on the stringy green grass that grew by the water's edge. I reached out into the water and scooped the jar full. Bringing it back I set it down in the cracked, dried mud that curled up by the shore of the pond. Dave and I watched as brown dirt swirled to the bottom of the jar. When the water cleared it revealed two plump tadpoles flicking their tails as they swam.

"All right!" I said. "We got two. Think I should try for some more?"

"Probably not," Dave said. "You might lose the tadpoles you've already caught."

"I guess you're right." As we stood up to go, I noticed a movement behind the bushy tree with the red berries where we'd found the two herdboys. "What's that over there?" I asked.

Dave looked. "I don't see anything."

"Look, there it is again," I said, pointing this time. "Line up your eyes with that branch on the left. It looks brown and . . . now it's gone."

"Was it an animal?" Dave asked.

"I don't think so," I answered. "It was almost like a shadow of a young boy."

Dave looked at me sharply. "You're not seeing ghosts are you?" he asked.

"I don't think so," I replied, "but it did look kind of spooky the way it disappeared so suddenly." A chill ran down my back.

"Let's get home," Dave said. "I don't want to be here anymore."

Both of us ran back to Rugendo, the memory of Ngugi dead on the ground and being carried limply to the hospital scorching images in my mind.

As the weeks went by, the memory faded. Kamau recovered, though Jon's dad never did figure out what had caused the sickness, or why Ngugi died and Kamau didn't. Ngugi's father had claimed Ngugi's body in a huff and refused to give permission for an autopsy. We thanked God for healing Kamau and went on with the business of school.

We Rhinos lived for the weekends. We enjoyed school, but how could we study when the sun shone and the forest surrounding the school practically shouted at us to visit?

We almost always played a game of soccer during morning recess. Matt chose sides one morning as usual and managed to put all of the Rhinos on his team.

"Can we play?" Jill, a girl from my fifth grade class, asked. Matt looked startled. Two new sixth grade girls knelt next to Jill as they tied up the shoelaces on their black soccer boots. They had a shiny new soccer ball beside them. Jill had honey-blonde hair, and I'd seen her score several goals in our fifth grade PE class.

"No way," Matt muttered, scowling. "We've already got even teams."

"Jill's pretty good at soccer," I suggested. "Maybe she could be on our team and the other girls could go on the other side."

"I said no!" Matt repeated, glaring at me. "Now let's play."

Jill shrugged her shoulders and said loudly to her friends, "Sorry, Rachel and Rebekah. It looks like the boys won't let us play. Too bad they don't know you played on a village soccer team in Zaire. Let's not waste our time with these losers." They moved away to an open bit of grass and passed their ball around.

I stared at the girls, amazed at their skillful touches. "Forget the girls, Dean," Matt growled. "We have a soccer game to play."

Jon kicked off to Matt. I stayed in the back where I played defense, not letting anyone dribble past my long legs. Matt, who scored goals like crazy as the center forward, passed the ball wide and raced forward. Jon swarmed like a bee toward the ball. Someone on the other team booted the ball to me. I trapped it and passed it to Dave who played center halfback. As I passed, Jon ran up to me. "What position are you playing?" I asked.

Jon smiled at me and said, "I don't play a position. I just love to kick the ball." With that, he sprinted up the field.

Dave gathered my pass at midfield. Like the center of the old black-and-white clock in our classroom, he rotated in a circle and calmly passed the ball to Matt. Matt pounced on the ball at pace and slammed it into the goal. "Yes!" he exulted. "I'm going to score a lot of goals this Saturday on titchie field day. We Stanleys are going to win as usual."

The bell rang to end recess. "What's titchie field day?" asked Jon.

"The way you hunt and hike, I think you've been here forever," Matt said. "I keep forgetting how new you are. Anyone from first to sixth grade at our school is called a titchie. It's from a British slang word, *titch,* meaning anything small or little. We're titchies and one Saturday each term we have titchie field day, a special day of games just for the titchies. There will be races, games, and other special events."

"How do I know which team I'm on?" Jon asked.

I stepped up to explain. "Our whole school is divided into two teams called Livingstones and Stanleys after the two famous African explorers. The first week of school they should have told you what team you're on."

"I wondered what that note meant, telling me I was a Stanley," Jon said. "I guess that means I'm on your team for titchie field day, Matt."

"Dean and I are Livingstones," Dave put in before turning to me. "Do you think we'll win titchie field day this time?" he asked.

We had both been at the school since first grade and had never won titchie field day. The Stanleys had a stranglehold on winning. "I hope so," I said, not sounding very hopeful.

Dave looked at me. "I don't think we have a chance," he said. "Jon's so fast he'll win all the races, and with Matt scoring goals in soccer, they'll win that for sure."

"Some of the Livingstone girls in our fifth grade class are pretty fast," I said. "Maybe they'll win some points."

"Like who?" Dave asked.

"Jill can run faster than most of the boys in fifth grade," I said. *Including me,* I thought, but I didn't have the courage to say it out loud.

"Are you starting to like Jill?" Dave frowned so his glasses lifted up on his nose.

"Of course not," I said, blushing.

Dave stared at me. "Just wondering," he stated. "First you suggest we let her play in our recess soccer game and now you're telling me what a great runner she is."

"We'd better hurry to class before we're late." I hastily changed the subject.

CHAPTER FOUR

TITCHIE FIELD DAY

The morning of titchie field day arrived bright and sunny. The day started with the sprints. As predicted, the Stanleys dominated, and Jon easily won both the fifty-yard dash and the hundred-yard dash followed by other Stanleys. Only the top three finishers in each race earned points for their team.

After the boys' races, one of the teachers carrying a clipboard announced the score with a handheld megaphone. As usual, it looked like a hopeless day for the Livingstones. The girls raced next. Dave and I stood to the side to watch. On this day we didn't hang around with Matt and Jon. We spotted them on the other side of the soccer field where the races took place. I only hated one thing about titchie field day. We Rhinos had to play against each other.

Jill easily won the fifty-yard dash. "All right, way to go, Jill!" I shouted.

Dave raised an eyebrow as he looked at me. "I thought you liked her," he said, nodding wisely.

"I'm just cheering for the Livingstones," I said, ignoring his teasing. But I did think Jill looked kind of cute, especially with her hair flying behind her as she ran.

As the teacher read off the score, we found the Livingstones had won all the points in the race. The two new girls from sixth grade who had wanted to join the soccer game with Jill came in second and third. "Hey, we might catch up," Dave said. "I didn't know Rebekah and Rachel were Livingstones."

As the girls lined up for the hundred-yard dash, Dave started cheering. I couldn't resist getting back at him. "So which one do you like, Dave? Rachel or Rebekah. You're cheering kind of loud."

"I'm just cheering for the Livingstones," he said. "Like you."

The next race started and, again, Jill and the two new girls swept the race. "That puts the Livingstones and Stanleys even," the teacher announced. Dave and I leaped around. Maybe this field day we'd have a chance. We'd never even been close before, and now we were tied.

The day went on with high jump and long jump. With a lot of help from the girls, the Livingstones stayed close. I even won third place in the high jump. Not because I jumped very high, but because one of the sixth grade Stanleys banged his knee on the bar and dropped out.

Then came the one event I dreaded. The rope climb. Each titchie had a chance to climb up the rope and win one point for his or her team. We formed a line in front of the rope. I hung back and watched as Dave scrambled up the rope.

I remembered the first time I'd tried this event in first grade, I thought it looked so easy. The other kids all scampered up like monkeys. I'd stood on the knot at the bottom of the rope, reached up with both hands and pulled. I expected my body to go up the rope. Nothing happened. I dangled there, horrified at my lack of ability to climb the rope. People had cheered and encouraged me, but I couldn't move up the rope. Finally I had dissolved into tears, let go of the rope, and gone to hide behind the crowd, trying to wipe away my embarrassment along with the tears.

Jon hoisted himself up the rope now as Matt urged him on. I shrunk back and let other, more eager kids push past me.

Usually the rope climb event was late in the day and the Stanleys were so far ahead it made no difference, but today we had a chance. Our winning of the field day could depend on how many Livingstones climbed the rope. Jill clambered up the rope. I decided I couldn't let my team down. I'd have to try. Besides, maybe I'd learned something in the four years since I'd failed to climb the rope in first grade.

Finally I could postpone it no longer. I stepped forward, grabbed the rope, and lifted my feet to the knot. So far, so good. I reached up with my arms, tightened my grip, and heaved. Nothing happened. I tried again and managed to pull myself up an inch with my arms. I began to turn red from the effort and the embarrassment. I struggled some more, but my long-legged body was too heavy for my arms.

I dropped off the rope and, gulping back the sobs that threatened to explode, I moved behind the crowd. I sniffed and dabbed at the tears that leaked out the corners of my eyes when someone said, "You did your best. That's all that matters. Thanks for trying." It was Jill. She'd seen me crying!

I cleared my throat. "Thanks," I managed to murmur.

The rope climb ended and the teacher stood up to announce the score. "The Stanleys are ahead by five points and there's only

THE POISON ARROW TREE

one event left. The boys' soccer game is worth twenty points to the winning team. So whoever wins the soccer game will win this titchie field day. Right now we'll have a one-hour break for lunch. The soccer game will start at the field at 2 P.M."

Dave and I ran to get in line for food at the senior store. The twelfth grade class always sold food during titchie field day— doughnuts, candy, hot dogs, hamburgers, soda pop. We each ordered a hamburger and a bottle of pop. We sat down under a purple-flowered jacaranda tree to eat. In front of us stretched the Great Rift Valley with Mt. Longonot, a dormant volcano with a gaping crater, planted in the middle of the valley. Rugendo Mission had been built on the side of the eastern wall of the Rift Valley, which my dad said was the largest scar on the earth's surface. As we ate, Jill came up with Rachel and Rebekah. "Can we eat with you guys?" she asked.

Dave kind of froze up and couldn't answer. So I said, "Sure."

"Have you met Rebekah and Rachel?" Jill asked. Both Dave and I shook our heads. Conversation with girls wasn't something we had practiced before, and we weren't too good at it.

"They're new in school this year. Their parents work in Zaire translating the Bible. They've been home schooled in Zaire. So even though they're a year apart in age, they're both in sixth grade."

"So, how's the hunting in Zaire?" I asked.

Rachel looked at Rebekah. "I don't know," she said. "We've never gone hunting."

Having exhausted our topics of conversation, Dave and I went back to eating and swigging. We finished eating in silence. Dave and I stood up. "We've got to go play the soccer game," I said.

"Hey, look," Dave pointed. "That family left six pop bottles under the tree. We can grab them and turn them in for the re-fund." He ran over and swooped up the bottles. As we headed to senior store to exchange the bottles for cash, we hunted around like vultures for any other stray bottles. We picked up another four bottles and pocketed the cash.

"We found enough bottles to buy a couple of candy bars to celebrate our victory," Dave said to the girls as we passed them. "We'll buy them after the soccer game."

"That's right. If you win the game, the Livingstones will win titchie field day for the first time I can remember," Jill said.

"Yeah," I answered. Dave was already walking away.

"Well, I'll be cheering for you," Jill said, smiling at me.

"Thanks." My head felt dizzy like a balloon had been inflated inside. I walked quickly to catch up with Dave.

"Why are you trembling, man?" Dave must have noticed my excitement.

"I don't know."

"It's the girls. Come on, Dean, focus. We have a soccer game to play, and you're shaking because some girl talked to you."

"She smiled," I started.

"Soccer, Dean. Come on! We have to win."

Dave's words brought me back to reality, but I couldn't help but wonder if maybe Jill liked me a little.

Our Livingstone team captain called us over to get set for the game. "I'm in goal," he said. "Dean, you play fullback and, Dave, you're our center halfback." The whistle blew and Matt kicked off for the Stanleys. They worked the ball up quickly using short tri-angle passes. Jon predictably ran in and started dribbling the ball. Matt slipped to the middle, just inside the goalkeeper's box. As

Jon crossed it to him, I stepped forward, cut off the pass, and kicked it to Dave. Dave turned to pass it upfield, but our center forward missed the trap and the Stanleys had the ball again.

We were pushed back against our goal most of the game. We just didn't have any good players up front to keep the ball and score. Dave and I played our hearts out, but the Stanleys outplayed us. The goalpost became our twelfth player. In the last five minutes, Matt hit the post after faking me out and firing on goal. I scrambled after the rebound and kicked the ball down the hill.

We only had one ball, so we got to rest when it rolled down the steep hill. Dave came over, panting. "Our forwards are never going to score. I'm going upfield to get a goal," he whispered to me. "Do your best to boot the ball up to me. It's our only chance."

Jon, who'd run down the hill to get the ball, got ready to take the throw-in. I stood near Matt, hoping to cut off the pass. Sure enough, Jon threw it straight to Matt. Matt leaned back into me, protecting the ball. I wasn't too worried because Matt couldn't shoot with his back to the goal. Matt passed the ball back to Paul, one of his players in the middle of the field, right where Dave should have been, but Dave had gone upfield. Before any of our defenders could cover him, Paul trapped the ball, took two steps, and slammed the ball at the goal. I turned and ran toward the goal to help cover. Our goalie dove to his left to block it. The shot was too hard for him to catch, but he punched it out. The ball rocketed off his fist right at my face. Before I could react the ball smacked my forehead and flew straight into our own goal. I had scored for the Stanleys! I couldn't believe it!

I stood stunned. I didn't know what to say. I felt like crying, but how many times can a guy cry on one lousy field day? I bit my lower lip and blinked back the tears. Dave came back and patted my shoulder. "It's OK, Dean. Let's see if we can get the tying goal."

But my heart wasn't in it. A few minutes later the final whistle shrieked in my ear. I felt miserable. Our one chance to win titchie field day and I had lost the soccer game with my own goal.

Matt and Jon both came over to shake my hand. "Good game, Dean," Matt said. "Sorry about the goal."

My tongue stuck to the back of my throat. I just nodded. I didn't have anything to say.

"Come on," Jon said, "I'll buy you a Coke. We may be Livingstones and Stanleys today, but the rest of the time we're the Rhinos and we're together."

Jill walked by. "Good try, Dean," she said. "Maybe Livingstones will never win titchie field day." The sad look on her face oozed disappointment.

"Thanks," I replied. I looked down at the ground.

Jon ordered the sodas. The senior reached elbow deep into the ice-cold water in the big metal cooler and pulled out the dripping bottles of Coca-Cola, made in Kenya and even sweeter than the American version. With a brisk motion of his hand he used the can opener to flick off the bottle lids with an explosive pop. The caps floated end over end and landed on the cracked cement. We each grabbed our bottle caps and peeled back the plastic foam lining from inside to see if we'd won a prize in the latest bottlers' promotion. We each had soccer balls inscribed inside the caps, but none was colored with red and black, so we didn't win any prizes.

Dr. Freedman, Jon's dad, swept up to the store, his white coat swinging out behind him. He looked anxious. He came over and asked, "Did I miss your game, Jon?"

"Yeah, Dad," Jon said, "but that's OK. We won, but it was really close."

"I'm sorry," he said. "I was on the way when they brought Kamau back into the hospital. Do you remember him? He was the boy you found near the pond."

"We remember him, Dad," Jon said. "I thought you said he got better."

"He did," Dr. Freedman said. "We sent him home several weeks ago. Now his parents brought him back. He suddenly got very sick this morning."

"Is it the same sickness?" Matt asked.

"That's what's so strange," Dr. Freedman said. "The symptoms are completely different so it can't be. We're doing tests, but we can't seem to find the cause of this sickness either. Your praying helped save him the last time. I want you boys to pray again."

CHAPTER FIVE

THE WITCH DOCTOR'S CURSE

"That's strange that Kamau is so sick again," Matt said as Jon's dad walked away.

"Makes it kind of hard to celebrate our victory," Jon said. Seeing my face he went on quickly, "I mean here we are concerned about who wins a day's worth of games and Kamau may die."

I sighed. "Yeah, I guess you're right. I still feel bad for losing the field day with my own goal, but when I think of someone like Kamau being so sick, it kind of puts things in perspective."

"*Perspective?* What kind of word is that? Is that like sweat?" Matt demanded.

He scratched his head as if thinking. "No, I guess that's *perspiration.* We had it on our vocabulary test last week."

I knew Matt was trying to joke me out of feeling bad. I decided to let him. I stood up and punched him on the shoulder. "You know what I mean. I may be feeling sorry for myself for losing a soccer game and a field day, but at least I'm alive and healthy. Come on. Let's get out of here."

"Yeah, let's go for a hike," Jon suggested. "Did anyone check our genet cat trap today?"

No one had. Since we had set up the trap we hadn't caught anything, and we had lost the enthusiasm of rising with the sun and the tropical birds to check the trap.

We traipsed into the forest, field day almost forgotten, and Kamau's sickness only a small dark cloud nagging in our minds.

Jon led the way followed by Matt. Dave and I were the tail-end-Charleys. Dave limped.

"Are you all right?" I asked.

"I think so," Dave answered. "I hit someone's ankle pretty hard in the soccer game when I went for the ball. It feels like I have a nasty bruise on my instep. I'm just walking carefully, that's all."

I slowed down to Dave's pace. He looked up. "It sure is peaceful down here under all these trees."

I nodded. The pillarlike trees and deep shadows made me think of a gothic cathedral we'd visited when traveling through Europe. "Maybe that's why in the African traditional religions they felt that spirits lived in certain trees."

"That's a weird thought, Dean," Dave said. "Where'd you come up with that?"

"My dad did some research on it for his magazine. Africans often made sacrifices and worshiped ancestral spirits under trees. Dad said they'd pour out beer and leave food to make their ancestors happy. They'd ask the ancestors to talk to God for them. I don't know why, but when you talked about how peaceful it was down here, the picture of Africans worshiping under trees popped into my mind."

"Hurry up, you guys, or we'll never get there," Matt called.

Dave and I picked up the pace, but Dave winced, especially on downhill sections when he had to put a lot of pressure on his foot to keep from slipping down the slope.

As we came close to our trap site, Jon motioned to us to be quiet. He crept up on the trap, disturbing the ground as little as possible. He came back shaking his head. "Nothing has even come near the trap," he announced.

"Maybe we should move the trap somewhere else," Matt suggested.

"Even more important than that, we need to put in fresh bait. The peanut butter has dried on the stick, and it's so hard and gray that I think a genet cat would rather throw up its lunch than take a bite," Jon said, wrinkling his nose with disgust.

"I didn't bring anything for bait," I said. No one else had either.

"We'll have to come back another day with new bait," Matt decided.

"Maybe a fish head," I suggested. "My dad often goes fishing at Lake Naivasha and catches bass."

"Sounds OK," Matt said, but I could tell he wasn't really interested. Building the trap had been a great idea, but since it hadn't caught anything right away he was ready to forget it. Matt liked things to happen right away. Waiting patiently for anything didn't agree with Matt.

"Let's go check our tree fort," Matt said, abruptly leading the way. "I feel like drinking some *chai*."

When he said that, Dave looked a bit funny. And as we walked he dragged further and further behind. At the tree house, Jon scrambled up the tree and threw down the hanging ladder. Matt climbed up first. We could hear him rattling our big black kettle where we kept tea leaves, sugar, and powdered milk for our *chai* drinks in the forest. "Hey," he yelled down. "There's no sugar left. How can we drink *chai* without sugar? What happened, Dave?"

Dave looked up timidly. He was treasurer and it was his job to take money from our club dues to buy supplies. "I forgot," he said. "I noticed the last time we had finished the sugar, but with school on and all, I just forgot. I'm sorry."

"Sorry doesn't quench my thirst, Dave," Matt said. Sometimes he could get really annoyed. "I was looking forward to a nice mug full of sweet milky tea. And don't suggest that we drink *ndubia*, tea without sugar. Makes me shiver to think of drinking that stuff."

"Don't be so hard on Dave," I defended. "We all make mistakes." Matt glared at me, but he stopped ripping on Dave.

Dave climbed up the ladder, wincing as he placed the instep of his sore foot on the rungs. Picking up the small wooden box with the padlock, he shook it, and we could hear coins rattling inside. "We have money in our box," Dave suggested. "Why don't we take out enough to buy sugar, go to the *duka*—"

"I'm in the mood to drink *chai* now," Matt cut in.

"You didn't let me finish," Dave said, calm as ever. "We can take out enough extra to buy a cup of *chai* and *mandazi* at the *chai* house while we're there buying the sugar. That way we can supply our tree house and have a good cup of *chai*. With *mandazi*, I might add, something you're not going to get here."

Matt could change moods quicker than a cobra could strike. He smiled. "Now that sounds like a good plan. All in favor, vote yes." We all voted yes. Dave removed the money from the box, we climbed down from the tree house, and set off for the *chai* house on the other side of Rugendo.

"*Muri ega?* Are you well?" the *chai* house owner greeted us in

Kikuyu as we sat down on the wobbly bench that lined the back wall behind a long table topped with wild-patterned Formica.

Matt, the only Rhino who really understood Kikuyu, answered for all of us, *"Ii. Turi ega.* Yes, we are well."* He ordered four mugs of *chai,* the sweet, milky Kenyan version of tea.

"Don't forget to buy some *mandazi,*" Jon prompted.

"Ongeza mandazi manne. Add four *mandazi,*" Dave said, counting out the shillings for the *chai* and four *mandazi*—square, deep-fried pastries kind of like doughnuts without holes but not nearly as sweet.

As we sucked noisily on our *chai* and dunked pieces of *mandazi* in the mugs to soften and sweeten them, two older Kikuyu men entered the *chai* house and sat down in the corner. Their foreheads wrinkled in concentration as they talked in hushed whispers.

I ignored them at first, savoring the *chai* and trying to forget my mistake in the soccer game. But the scene of heading the ball into our own goal kept repeating itself in my mind like my kid brother, Craig, rewinding and replaying his favorite parts of a cartoon on the video over and over.

The Kikuyu men became agitated and one began speaking louder. The *chai* mugs on the table rocked back and forth, and the old men's *chai* spilled over the rims of the mugs. A small river of the brown liquid headed toward our end of the long table. It was diverted by a crack in the Formica and dripped off the table to soak into the sawdust on the floor.

Matt's eyes opened up like someone who's suddenly seen a leopard in a tree. "What's the matter, Matt?" I asked. "Scared the *chai* was going to drip all over your shorts and leave an embarrassing wet mark?"

Matt's eyes blazed as he signaled for me to be quiet. He leaned forward and said very quietly, "Something important has come up. Finish your *chai* and *mandazi* as quickly as possible. Then let's get out of here. But act natural."

I couldn't figure what had gotten into Matt. I looked at Dave with a puzzled frown. He shrugged. I swirled the remaining *chai* in the bottom of my cup, watching bits of *mandazi* crumbs surfacing. I chugged it down and, in African fashion, gave a polite belch. We all stood up and thanked the *chai* house owner for the tea.

The two old men talked on, huddled together. They didn't notice our exit.

When we had gone a safe distance from the *chai* house Dave asked, "What's up, Matt? Why'd you make us leave so soon?"

"Didn't you hear those two men talking?" Matt asked.

We looked at each other. "Of course," Jon answered, "but I didn't understand a word of it. They were speaking in Kikuyu."

"I thought you guys could understand a little Kikuyu. Anyway, when they started speaking loudly and spilled their *chai,* one of the men said Kamau's sickness had been caused by a curse. It seems Ngugi's father called in a witch doctor who made the curse, and that's why Kamau is sick again. The old men were arguing about whether to pass the news on to the church leaders. One said yes. The other said they should ignore it. He said if Kamau died, it would be an even exchange and both families would forget the matter."

"This stuff is scary," said Jon. "Ngugi's father freaked me out that day in the hospital when he threatened to get his revenge on Kamau's family. We'd better go tell my dad."

We began running to Jon's house. As we ran up the driveway, lined by yellow and green century cactus plants with their long leaves lolling onto the ground like tongues from a tired-out dog, we saw Jon's dad picking lemons from his lemon tree.

"Dad, Dad," Jon burst out. "We just found out why Kamau's sick. Ngugi's father got a witch doctor to put a curse on him!"

CHAPTER SIX

DEMONIC ATTACK

Dr. Freedman stepped out from under his lemon tree and looked at us with a puzzled frown. "What did you say?" he asked.

"We said Kamau's sickness is caused by a witch doctor's curse. Ngugi's father went to the witch doctor to get his revenge on Kamau's family," Jon said urgently. "Come on, Dad, you've got to do something."

"Hold on, Jon," his dad said, chuckling. "Now, I know Kamau is very sick, but I doubt very much if a witch doctor has anything to do with it. Witch doctors just play on old tribal fears and superstitions. They use gimmicks like throwing bones. I watched one at work soon after we arrived here in Africa. He looked impressive. The child he was examining had small oozing sores all over his body. The witch doctor said he had discerned the cause of the disease. No one in the family had given a libation or offering to their deceased grandfather. He told the family they had to sacrifice a goat to the dead grandfather and plead with him to forgive them for not remembering him. When the ancestor was happy, they could then ask him to talk to God on their behalf to allow their child to be healed. The family brought the goat. The witch doctor did the sacrifice and said it was successful. He kept a large share of the goat meat and charged the family two chickens for his services."

"Well, what happened?" Jon asked.

"The child got better, but I had looked at the child closely. All he had was chicken pox. He'd have gotten better even without the sacrifice. So the witch doctor made out pretty well on that one. I think witch doctors are just fooling people. But, tell me, why do you boys think Kamau's sickness is caused by a witch doctor's curse? The African people are not very open about sharing that kind of stuff, especially not with missionaries or their kids."

"I overheard two older men talking about it in the *chai* house," Matt said. "They were arguing over whether to tell the church leaders or not. They sounded serious."

"Well, maybe I'll have Pastor Waweru check into it. Like I said, I don't really believe witch doctors have any power. Besides, Kamau and his family are faithful Christians. I don't think much will come of this, but we'll see what the chaplain finds out."

The next day I went to church with my parents. The service always seemed to last so long. They translated the sermon from Kikuyu to English. When the translator finished and the preacher went on in Kikuyu, I would tune out. I never managed to switch back on when the translator picked up again. I would phase out for five minutes or more. When I did listen again, I found I had missed something important. I'd get confused and turn off again.

This morning my mind kept going over and over the soccer game. I replayed it a hundred times in my mind, but in my mind's replay, I didn't knock the ball into our own goal. Instead I made a magnificent chest trap, turned, and passed the ball upfield to where

Dave waited. The pass sliced perfectly between the defenders, leading Dave into the keeper's box where he pounded the winning goal into the corner, just nicking the corner post.

Suddenly everyone stood up. They might have been cheering for Dave's goal, but it was only time for the last hymn. I hadn't learned anything from the sermon, but my daydreaming had made the time pass quickly. I looked over to where Matt and Jon sat. I sighed as I realized my daydreaming hadn't changed the score from the day before. We had still lost the game.

After church we Rhinos walked home together. We stopped off in the garden at Jon's house to pick some black raspberries. As we snaked our hands in between the thorn-cluttered branches to get the berries, we heard two men talking. Turning, I saw Dr. Freedman walking up the road with Pastor Waweru.

Matt signaled to all of us to get down. We crouched beside the berry bush and listened.

"This is a very serious matter, Dr. Freedman," Pastor Waweru said. "I went to see Ngugi's father. At first he denied calling in any witch doctor. I asked some of the neighbors and they confirmed that a well-known *mganga,* or witch doctor, had visited Ngugi's father. So I went back to him. This time he admitted he had called in the witch doctor, but he said it was none of our business. If Kamau died, it would prove Kamau's family had been to blame for Ngugi's death."

Dr. Freedman looked skeptical. "I still don't think the witch doctor has the power of life and death over Kamau."

"He doesn't," agreed Pastor Waweru, "but he is in touch with spiritual forces of the Wicked One, and these demonic forces do have the power to attack and bring sickness and even death. The

Bible confirms this, Dr. Freedman. Haven't you read Luke 13 about the woman in the synagogue who had been crippled by a spirit? When Jesus healed her on the Sabbath he said Satan had held the woman in bondage for eighteen years. And, of course, Job and his family were attacked by Satan. Job's children were killed."

"But that was years ago," Dr. Freedman began. "Surely, in this day and age—"

Pastor Waweru held his arms open wide as he interrupted, "In this day and age Satan is still alive and well. And his spiritual forces have much power. They have no more power than God allows them as we can see from the story of Job, but we give Satan and his demons all sorts of room to attack when we refuse to believe he even exists."

Jon reached out and plucked a black raspberry and popped it into his mouth. I decided to eat one, too, but a thorn raked my fingers. "Aii," I whispered.

Matt put his finger to his lips to silence me. He tilted to the side and a thorn stabbed his leg. He gasped, but didn't say anything.

Dr. Freedman stared at the raspberry bush for a second, then turned back to Pastor Waweru. "Of course I believe Satan exists," Dr. Freedman said. "But—"

"You say it with your mouth," Pastor Waweru cut in, "but to really believe in something you have to believe it in your head and your heart. You have to act on your belief. My people say, *Kusema na kufanya ni mambo tofauti,* 'to speak and to do are different matters.'" He turned to walk away.

"Wait," Dr. Freedman called. He hustled after the departing pastor and caught him by the shoulder. They talked, but we couldn't hear anything now that they had moved down the road. They soon returned to Jon's house. Dr. Freedman went in and came out a minute later with his car keys. The two men climbed into the Freedmans' Land Rover. The big diesel engine belched out a cloud of dark black smoke as it started up, then it bounced down the driveway.

We all looked at each other. "I wonder where they're going?" I asked.

"Probably to talk with Ngugi's father or something," Jon said. "Well, I haven't had lunch yet and nice as these berries are, they're not filling me up." He ran down to his house.

"Let's meet here at two and ride bikes," Matt called.

"All right," Jon said before he slammed the door.

"See you guys this afternoon," I said, heading to my house.

After a wonderful Sunday dinner with some roast warthog meat from my dad's recent hunting trip and mashed potatoes from our garden, plus a rhubarb pie with homemade ice cream, I felt so full I could hardly sit.

"May I be excused?" I asked. "Ah, that feels better," I said as I stretched out on the couch.

"Actually," my mom said, "there's an even better position after you've eaten too much—standing up over the sink and washing the dishes."

"Washing the dishes! Mom, can't they soak until tomorrow?"

She smiled patiently, but her answer was firm. "No."

Craig started clearing the dirty dishes. "Why do I always have to clear?" he whined.

"You could always swap with me," I said. "Washing is great fun. You can make bubbles in the water and slop water onto the floor and make everyone slip."

Craig brightened. "Can I?"

"No," my mom said. "Craig is not old enough to wash yet. Now get on with your work, Dean."

My dad said, "I'll dry the dishes. I'm supposed to be at an elders' meeting at church, but it won't start for another half hour."

As we worked side by side, I asked, "Dad, did you hear about Kamau?"

"I heard he was sick again and they couldn't figure out what was wrong."

I decided to tell him what we'd overheard in the *chai* house. "We Rhinos heard Kamau's sickness was caused by a witch doctor's curse."

My dad turned immediately. "Where'd you hear this?"

"Matt overheard two old men talking at the *chai* house yesterday."

"Yesterday! Why didn't you tell me right away?"

"We did tell Dr. Freedman, but he didn't think it was important. So we didn't tell anyone else."

"Dr. Freedman didn't do anything about it?" my dad asked.

"Well, he said he would talk to Pastor Waweru and today we heard them talking about it near the Freedman's house. Pastor Waweru said he'd found out there really had been a witch doctor involved, but Dr. Freedman still didn't think it had much to do with Kamau's sickness. They argued a bit and then drove off in the Freedmans' Land Rover."

Dropping his dishtowel, my dad said, "I've got to talk to him right away. Let's go."

Happy to leave the dishes, I hurriedly dried my hands and followed him.

"Honey, what about the dishes?" my mom called after us.

"We'll take care of them later. There's an emergency!" my dad answered.

At Jon's house we found Mrs. Freedman cleaning up after their meal. Jon didn't have to help. She had left one clean plate on the table. "Where'd your husband go?" my dad asked.

"He and Pastor Waweru went to visit some family about a mile away. I'm not sure where." She didn't look very happy. "He hardly ever sits down for a meal with us anymore." She sighed. "He said he'd be back soon so I'm keeping his food hot."

Just then Dr. Freedman drove up in his Land Rover. As he walked in the door shaking off the dust, he looked scared, just like Matt had looked the time he'd tripped on the edge of a steep ravine and his coat had snagged on a thorny lion's paw tree, keeping him inches away from a twenty-foot drop.

My dad walked over to him. "Are you all right?"

Dr. Freedman nodded. "Yeah, I think so." He sat down shakily. His wife looked concerned.

"What's wrong, Dad?" Jon asked.

"I've just come face-to-face with deep, bitter rage," he said slowly, carefully.

"What do you mean?" my dad asked.

Taking a deep breath, Dr. Freedman told my dad what we Rhinos had overheard about the witch doctor. "At first I didn't believe it was anything serious, but today Pastor Waweru opened my eyes to the fact that Kamau could be suffering from some sort of demonic attack. So we went to see Ngugi's father. He told us Kamau would die because he had asked a witch doctor to unleash powerful spiritual forces against him. I told him he should stop. I said Kamau's family had nothing to do with Ngugi's death."

"What happened next?" my dad asked.

Dr. Freedman shook his head. "I've never seen anyone so angry. His eyes rolled, his body literally shook with anger. He seemed to be consumed, controlled by his anger. I've never seen anything like it. It frightened me. He told me I was abusing him. Not only would Kamau die, but he would call in the witch doctor this very afternoon and bring another curse on someone else here at Rugendo. Then he marched away.

"Pastor Waweru said we had to pray. That was the only answer. So I dropped him off at the church elders' meeting and they said they would be praying. But I don't know. I'm so confused. How can a witch doctor's curse bring on physical sickness? Sickness and disease are caused by germs, bugs, worms, not by some traditional African spirits."

My dad put his arm on Dr. Freedman's shoulder. "There's more to this than you understand. Actually, Pastor Waweru had the right answer. We have to pray. I'm going over to meet with the church elders, and we'll see how to handle this."

"Thanks," Dr. Freedman said, looking drained.

"It's new and scary for you to meet up with the powers of darkness like this," my dad said. "Don't worry. In the name of Jesus we have the power and the victory."

After my dad left, I said to Jon, "Let's ride our bikes."

"I don't know," said Jon. "My head just started to ache."

A FRIGHTENING SICKNESS

"**M**aybe you'd better rest, Jon," his dad said without looking up from his plate of food.

"Yeah, I'll see you later, Jon," I said. "I hope you feel better." I slipped out of the house.

I met Matt and Dave, and we rode bikes for a while, but it wasn't the same without Jon. He usually rode like crazy, dodging between trees and making jumps over—and into—ditches. Matt, a wild driver himself, could always count on Jon to keep our rides exciting. Dave and I didn't like bike accidents, so we didn't keep up like Matt wanted.

"I'm bored," Matt announced. "Let's do something different."

"Like what?" I asked, not sure what to expect.

Matt thought for a while. He jumped up. "I've got it. We can have a faith ride. You know, like the faith walk we had at youth group last Sunday night. It's where you close your eyes and trust your partner to guide you by voice commands. Only we can do it riding our bikes. Dave, you go first. Dean, you be second, and I'll go last."

I looked at Dave. He didn't look very excited about the idea, but neither of us wanted to tell Matt no.

"Let's go to that circle next to the mission guest house," Matt said. "That will make it challenging and exciting at the same time. It will be hard to ride a bike around the traffic circle with your eyes closed, and if you go off the road, you"—I noticed how he kept saying "you"—"might ride off the steep bank on the one side or into the drainage ditch on the other side. Man, what a great idea!"

We followed Matt like chickens on the way to the chopping stump. At the circle Matt got off his bike. "OK, Dave, close your eyes and start riding. We'll tell you when and where to turn."

Dave's face looked the color of cow gum, the rubber cement my dad used at his office for laying out pages of his magazine. He pushed off and made his way unsteadily around the circle, following our shouted directions of, "Left! Left! No, now turn right! Watch out for the ditch! Left, we said!"

After Dave successfully negotiated the circle, Matt motioned to me. I got on my bike and started. I was terrified. I could hear the shouted instructions, but I imagined I was headed for the bank or the ditch so I opened my eyes slightly to see where I was. To my amazement I was actually on the road. I closed my eyes again and forced myself to follow Matt's and Dave's directions, but I kept peeking, just to be sure.

When I finished, Matt said with disgust, "You guys went around like a couple of pansies. Let me show you how to really ride in faith." He hopped on his bike and pedaled like crazy. Dave and I managed to say left once, but Matt was going so hard and fast toward the bank that we froze. Matt started to shout. "Which way do I turn? Come on, which way?"

He looked so funny steaming toward the bank with his eyes

shut tight that Dave and I started to giggle and couldn't tell him anything. Matt flew off the edge of the road and tumbled spokes-over-tennis-shoes down the bank.

We ran over to where Matt rubbed his head as he pulled himself out from under his bent bike. "Why didn't you tell me to turn? You guys are just a bunch of baboons."

Dave got to him first. "Ouch," Matt said, gently touching a lump on his forehead. "That hurts."

Dave helped him stand up, and they examined his various cuts, wounds, and scratches. "Now we're all wounded," Dave said. "I've got a sore foot and you've got bumps and bruises. Jon has a headache."

"What about me?" I asked.

"You have a sore heart after yesterday's game," Matt said. Then he saw my face. "Hey, I'm sorry," he apologized.

I gripped Matt's front wheel between my knees and straightened out the handlebars. Matt bent over and ripped out the one spoke that had come loose. "I'm sure it will ride just as well without one spoke," Matt said. We rode by Jon's house to see how he was feeling. His mom answered the door.

"How's Jon?" Matt asked.

"I'm afraid he's gotten a high fever to go along with his headache," she answered. "Thanks for coming by. I'll tell him you were here. What happened to you, Matt?"

"Just a slight bike wreck," Matt smiled. He always liked to bask in visible injuries. "I'll be fine."

"I hope Jon gets better," Dave said. And we left.

The next morning, Jon was not in school. At lunch I heard from my parents that Jon had been put in the hospital. His fever was dangerously high. "They're doing the blood test for malaria," Mom said, "but I doubt it will show anything. The Freedmans haven't been away from Rugendo in two months and at eight thousand feet this place is too high for mosquitoes."

That night I heard that even though the test for malaria had been negative they were treating Jon for the disease anyway. In our family devotions I asked if we could pray for both Jon and Kamau. My dad agreed.

"Dear Lord," I prayed, "please help Jon and Kamau to get better. I don't know what kind of sickness they have, but I know you are God. Help them. In Jesus' name, Amen."

Craig's five-year-old prayer was even shorter. "Dear Jesus, make Jon and Kamau get better. Amen."

Mom and Dad both prayed like typical grown-ups and went on for a long time. They prayed something I hadn't heard them pray before. They prayed about putting on God's armor. They prayed God's protection over Jon and Kamau in the name of Jesus and by the power of his blood. They also asked God to bind Satan and his forces.

"Why did you pray like that?" I asked when they were done. "All that stuff about God's armor and the power of his blood."

My dad explained, "We really believe that both Kamau's and Jon's sickness are caused by evil spirits, so we prayed spiritual warfare types of prayers."

"What's spiritual warfare?" I asked.

"When Paul wrote to the Christians at Ephesus, he told them we Christians are in a spiritual battle." He reached over for his well-worn Bible and flipped quickly toward the end. "Here's what it says in Ephesians 6:12." I balanced on my stomach on the back of the couch and looked over his shoulder. The verse had been heavily underlined with a red felt-tip marker. He read, "'For our struggle is not against flesh and blood, but against the rulers, against the authorities, against the powers of this dark world and against the spiritual forces of evil in the heavenly realms.'" He looked up. "It goes on from there and talks about putting on God's spiritual armor so we can stand against Satan. So I was just praying like a soldier getting ready for the battle. The battle is constant and we all should wear the armor all the time, but we Christians often forget we're living in a war zone. Times like this when we face real spiritual danger remind me to pray on the armor piece by piece."

Fear gripped my heart like an icy hand. "You don't think Jon is going to die, do you?"

Dad's face looked grim. "I don't know," he said, "but knowing that witch doctor had put some sort of curse on Kamau and now with Jon sick right after he promised to curse someone else at Rugendo, I know we've got a battle on our hands. God tells us that the victory is ours, but we must be alert and pray."

"But why Jon?" I asked.

Dad looked at me. "I'm not sure. I do know Satan often attacks those who are the most weak and vulnerable. Sometimes it is the child in a family. Other times it's a person who has not confessed some sin in their life. Unconfessed sin can leave a hole in our armor that Satan can penetrate. That's why one of the pieces of armor listed here in Ephesians 6 is the breastplate of righteousness."

He showed me the picture in his study Bible of a Roman soldier wearing his armor. "None of us is righteous on our own," he went on. "We all have sinned, but when we believe in Jesus, God forgives us and cleanses us. God looks at us and sees us as righteous because we are covered by Jesus' blood. We are forgiven. That's our righteousness."

"But what happens if we sin?" I asked. "I try not to, but sometimes I get angry, like this morning when Craig scarfed up the last piece of toast before I got to the breakfast table."

Dad smiled. "When we sin as Christians, all we need to do is confess and God has promised in 1 John 1:9 to forgive our sins and clean us up. By examining our lives every day we can see where we've sinned and confess and pull the breastplate back on before it slips and gives Satan an opportunity to attack."

Dad's mini-sermon kind of went beyond me. I had to have him help me reconstruct what he said when writing this story up for our Rugendo Rhino records. But it made me feel grown-up to have my dad talk to me like that. And I had an understanding of the seriousness of Jon's sickness.

The next day we heard that Jon and Kamau were both worse. Their fevers soared. Malaria medicine hadn't done anything. They could find no physical cause for the sicknesses and their bodies stubbornly refused to respond to any treatment. At lunchtime my dad told me the church elders had called an all-station prayer meeting for that evening to deal with the spiritual attack on Rugendo.

"Can I come?" I asked.

Mom shook her head, but Dad paused and said, "Yes. We have the right to claim protection over you. Just make sure all your sins are confessed and up-to-date."

I spent most of the afternoon thinking through different things I had done wrong, confessing them to God and asking for his forgiveness. I also had to ask Craig to forgive me for teasing him and bullying him. "And I'm especially sorry for taking the nylon stockings out of your soft toy monkey that Mom made for you and giving them to our puppies," I said.

At the prayer meeting I sat with my parents. Most of the missionaries came in with worried looks on their faces. There were a few whispered greetings. One of the men started the meeting by leading in some hymns while we waited for others to arrive. Jill came in with her parents, but I didn't see any other kids. A white-haired lady played the battered old upright piano in the front of the station meeting hall. After about ten minutes Pastor Waweru arrived with a group of Kenyans. Most of them were church elders. The church pastor was there along with the headmaster of the Kenyan high school and Kamau's parents. Kamau's father gripped an old leather cap in his hands while his wife dabbed at her eyes with a flowered handkerchief. My dad got up and welcomed the Kenyans, ushering them to seats near the front.

He stood in front of the group. "As you know," he said, "we've called this meeting to pray for young Kamau and Jon Freedman. They're both very sick with no apparent cause except that we hear a witch doctor has put a curse on them at Ngugi's father's request. Most of you will remember that Ngugi is the boy who died earlier this month."

A grim picture filled my mind of Kamau and Ngugi laid out in the grass.

My dad went on, "We feel the sicknesses are linked to some sort of spiritual attack, and we as a group of Christians must get on our knees before God and pray and win this battle. I've asked Pastor Waweru to give us some background on the nature of spiritual warfare in this area. I know some of us from the West are less likely to believe in the power of spiritual forces."

"That's where I have a question," said Mr. Edwards, a tomato-faced missionary who showed Christian films in the area. "I believe in Satan and his power, but if Jon and Kamau are both believers and their parents are believers, how can Satan touch them? I agree we need to pray, but I don't feel this is a spiritual attack."

"Fair enough," my dad answered. "That's why I've asked Pastor Waweru to speak to us first. We need to be united in prayer."

My dad stepped aside and Pastor Waweru stood up. He started with a short prayer of blessing. "Satan has power," he said, with a smile, "but Jesus Christ has much more power! That's our assurance tonight."

The station intercom phone rang. The lady who answered it waved Dr. Freedman over. I watched him talk on the phone at the back of the room. I could see his face wrinkle into a frown as he listened. He almost dropped the phone. He hung up and said with a choking voice, "Jon and Kamau are both having trouble breathing. Please keep praying. I have to go see what we can do, but it looks like they're near the end." Tears glistened in his eyes as he ran out the door.

CHAPTER EIGHT

SPIRITUAL WARFARE PRAYING

I listened intently as Pastor Waweru led the prayer meeting. This time my mind didn't wander even a little bit.

"We do need to pray," he said, "but we must be prepared first. Satan's forces, demons, do have power, but the Bible shows us they are under Christ's authority."

I shifted in my seat, uneasy with the talk about demons.

"In the past we Africans lived in fear of spiritual forces. My father was a young boy when the first missionaries came. He used to tell me the most important thing those first missionaries taught us was that if we believed in Jesus we had power against spiritual attacks. That's why so many people came to Christ. We weren't running to a Western religion. We were running for safety. My father and the other early church leaders around Rugendo learned how to stand firm."

"But how can we be sure this is a spiritual attack?" harped Mr. Edwards. "I've always understood that believers can't be hurt by Satan."

Pastor Waweru nodded and answered, "Sometimes it is hard to

know when a sickness is caused by spiritual forces or some physical illness." He smiled. "We Africans tend to say sickness always has a spiritual cause. That is our cultural understanding. You Christians from the West usually blame some physical cause such as a virus or a germ. In this case we know spiritual forces have been called on to bring the sicknesses. And Christians can be vulnerable to satanic attack. Ephesians 4:26–27 says if we leave anger in our hearts overnight we give the devil a foothold."

A shiver ran down my back. What if I got angry with Craig again and forgot to ask forgiveness?

Pastor Waweru went on. "A foothold means a place where Satan can get a grip on us. So unconfessed sin can leave a gap in our spiritual armor, and, as a result, Satan can hurt Christians."

My dad cut in, "We also have to remember that Jesus told Peter, who believed in Jesus, that Satan wanted to sift Peter like wheat. And Job, a God-fearing man, was also attacked by Satan in a test of his faith. Satan has no more power than God allows, or than we Christians allow by leaving sin in our lives."

Pastor Wawero nodded. "That's why the first step in spiritual warfare praying is for all of us to confess our sins and claim back any territory we've given over to Satan. Then we can go on and claim the victory." He read some verses from the Psalms. "Each person must pray silently, asking God to examine his or her own heart." I had a hard time keeping my eyes closed, and noticed a lot of people crying.

After a few minutes Pastor Waweru said, "If you have to speak with someone and ask forgiveness, do it now." I heard rustling and peeked again. Quite a few people walked over to others, gave hugs, and whispered to each other.

My dad led everyone through the spiritual armor from Ephesians 6, explaining why it was important for each person to have each piece of armor in place, and stopping so we could pray and protect ourselves.

"Now we need to praise the Lord," Dad said. "King Jehoshaphat knew the importance of praise in battle. In 2 Chronicles 20 when he went out to battle, he put the singers in front of the soldiers. As they began to sing and praise, God set ambushes against the enemy and Israel won the battle. Let's praise the Lord in song and watch his answer." We spent some time singing praise songs. I thought the roof might shake off the building.

There followed a powerful time of prayer with Kenyans and missionaries alike calling on God to act and save Kamau and Jon. Prayers binding Satan and his demons. Prayers of confession. Prayers reminding God of his promises. Prayers of praise. Strong warfare prayers. I'd never heard such prayers and I just knew God would answer.

After almost two hours of praying, Dr. Freedman opened the door and walked in. The prayers hushed. Everyone turned. Dr. Freedman struggled to speak. Finally he managed, "I think we're going to lose them. Nothing we've done makes any difference." Kamau's parents came over to him along with Mrs. Freedman. "We're going to the hospital to be with our boys." The grieving parents held onto each other as they walked out of the meeting hall.

My eyes caught Jill's, who had turned around to listen to Dr. Freedman. Her face looked as frightened as a tiny dik-dik antelope caught in the headlights of a car.

No one spoke. "Looks like we've failed," Mr. Edwards said.

Dad stood up. "The battle is not over yet. We must continue praying with faith and believe. We can't retreat yet. I'm sure we are making progress. This is not a physical illness. It is spiritual, and we need to pray on to victory. I suggest we close this meeting and the pastors and elders and any others who feel up to it can go down to the hospital and pray at the bedside of the two boys until the victory is won. Everyone else can go on home, but keep praying. This type of prayer needs a lot of support."

After the final prayer, the meeting broke up. "Can I go to the hospital and pray with you?" I asked Dad as he shrugged his coat on.

He leaned over and his steady brown eyes filled my vision. Finally he said, "I know you want to be with your friend, Dean, but this might not be an easy time. I think it would be best if you went home with Mom. But keep praying."

"What if Jon dies? I never got a chance to say good-bye."

He gripped me firmly on the shoulder. "I'm sorry, Dean, but I want you to go home. You can pray there."

I nodded and walked home with my mom, the flashlight cutting jerkily through the darkness. I planned to keep on praying in my room, but as soon as I started, I nodded off. I shook my head to wake up and prayed for another minute but then I fell asleep. I couldn't help it.

When I woke in the morning I realized I'd failed. I had slept instead of praying for Kamau and Jon. As I stumbled down the stairs, the heavy aroma of perked Kenyan coffee filled the kitchen. I found Mom and Dad sitting at the dining room table eating toast and drinking coffee. Dad had gray pockets under his eyes and his beard stubble made him look a lot older, but he was smiling.

"Good news!" he said. "Kamau and Jon are getting better! God answered our prayers!"

"What happened?" I asked, feeling relieved. I sat down as Mom popped two slices of bread into the toaster.

"We were up for hours last night. We made a circle around Jon's and Kamau's beds and started praising and praying. It felt like we'd moved into the very presence of God. Those Kenyan pastors really know how to pray."

"I tried to pray in bed, but I fell asleep," I confessed. I peeled a bright yellow finger banana and shoved it into my mouth.

"We all felt exhausted, Dean. We bound any demonic forces and commanded them to leave in the name of Jesus. Suddenly it seemed like a spirit of peace fell on the room like a blanket. I can't really explain it. We knew God's presence was right there. As we fell silent, praying only in our hearts, we could literally see both Kamau and Jon start to breathe more easily. Dr. Freedman was the most surprised. I think he'd given up hope. He felt the boys and said the fever had broken on both of them. We couldn't stop praying then. We had to thank God and praise him for winning the victory just as he promised." He sniffed. "What's that smell?"

"The toast!" Mom jumped up. Smoke curled out of the toaster. The automatic popper-upper had burned out the year before. She grabbed the two charred slices, opened the window, and flung them outside. Our dog, Grump, eagerly gobbled them up and sat back on her haunches, hoping for more.

PINEWOOD DERBY

That afternoon after school we visited Kamau and Jon in the hospital. Matt smuggled in two bottles of Sprite and Jon and Kamau sucked on the straws thirstily. "I'm glad you guys made it through the night," Matt said.

"We'll miss you at school," I said. Jon just nodded. Kamau smiled, but neither had the strength to answer.

"We'll come by and visit again," Dave said as we left.

Two days later, Matt and Dave came by my house before school. "Do you remember what day today is?" Matt asked.

I frowned. "I'm not sure."

"It's the day we get our kits for Pinewood Derby. Boy, do I have the greatest plan worked out. I'm going to make a Toyota Celica Safari Rally car," Dave said excitedly.

"That's right!" I said. "Pinewood Derby! I'd clean forgotten about it with Jon and Kamau being sick. I have no idea what kind of car I'll make."

"Me neither," said Matt, "but I know mine will be fast." Matt never spent too much time with the finer parts of sanding and painting. His car always looked like a block of wood. He concentrated on the wheels. And his cars were always fast.

"We'd better remember to pick up a kit for Jon," I said. "I'm sure he can get started on it as he gets better."

"Maybe we could get a kit for Kamau, too," Dave suggested.

"Good idea!" Matt confirmed.

After we sat down for chapel, loud clapping prevented the school woodshop teacher from giving his announcement. Those of us who had been at school for more than one year knew he would tell us when and where to pick up our Pinewood Derby kits after school. In our excitement we started clapping and cheering. The teacher stood smiling shyly, one hand waving in a vague attempt to get us to quiet down. Our cheering gradually subsided. To kick off his announcement, he showed us a beautiful Model-T Ford he had made for last year's Pinewood Derby. He went on to explain what the Pinewood Derby was all about.

"The Pinewood Derby is a car race, but first you have to build the cars. Everyone who enters will receive a kit." The teacher held up a car kit, which consisted of a rectangular block of wood, two axles, four plastic wheels, and four nails to hold the wheels on the axles.

"You each draw the design you want on your block of wood. We'll post times when you can come to the woodshop after school to get help cutting your blocks with our electric saws. After that you'll have to sand your car, making it as smooth as possible before painting."

The actual Pinewood Derby race would take place on a Saturday, just over three weeks away. Even though I'd heard the announcement every year, it still excited me and made me want to get out there and win. I'd never won any awards. Not for workmanship, that's for sure. I had a hard time doing things neatly. Dave, on the other hand, had won a trophy the year before for workmanship. His cars always looked *safi*, our slang word for anything really cool. My dad told me in Swahili it just meant "clean."

After school Matt, Dave, and I went to the woodshop at the appointed time to pick up our kits. "Can we have a kit for Jon as well?" Matt asked.

"Sure," the teacher answered. "I heard he's getting better. The Lord really answers prayer, doesn't he? But Jon won't be back in school yet, will he?"

"I don't think so," Matt said, "but maybe if he has the kit he can look at it and plan how he's going to make his car when he comes back to school."

"We also want a kit for Kamau," Matt said.

The woodshop teacher scratched his stubbly chin. "I'm not sure. Kamau isn't a student here."

"We know," Dave answered, "but after all our prayers for him and Jon, our Rhino club wanted to buy him a kit as well."

The woodshop teacher smiled. "I understand. Here's a kit for Kamau as well."

We stopped by the hospital. We peeped through the small window in the door before pushing it open. "How are you guys today?" Matt ventured.

"I'm feeling better," Jon said and yawned. "Just tired. I feel more tired than the day we tried to run all the way up Mt. Longonot. How about you, Kamau?"

Kamau smiled and nodded. "Yes, I'm feeling much better. And I wanted to thank you."

"For what?" I asked, wondering if he'd seen the car kits Dave and I held behind our backs.

"For praying. My dad said that if people hadn't prayed I'd have probably died. And Jon, too."

"It's God who answered our prayers," I said, "and we're all thankful for that."

"Yeah, we're glad you're both better," Dave said.

"We brought you a present," Matt said. Dave and I pulled out the plastic bags with the Pinewood Derby kits.

"What's this block of wood?" Jon asked.

Kamau turned his kit upside down and shook out the axles and wheels onto the blue hospital blanket.

"These are Pinewood Derby kits," Dave explained and told them about the upcoming race.

"Each age-group races against each other. It's a good thing you guys aren't in sixth grade or you wouldn't have a chance of winning," boasted Matt. "My car will be pure speed."

"What design are you going to make?" Dave asked all of us.

"I'm not sure," Matt said, "but it'll be fast."

Jon squinted at his block of wood as if picturing what his car would look like. "I want mine to be aerodynamically shaped," Jon said, "maybe like a Porsche 911 sports car."

"I thought I'd make mine look like a Toyota Celica. I have a picture of Bjorkman from the last Safari Rally, and I'm going to make mine look like that," said Dave. "What about you, Dean?"

"Well, I was thinking of making mine look like a banana. I thought it might win a prize for creativity and still go kind of fast."

The others eyed me as if I was a monkey that had just jumped down out of a tree. I could tell they didn't think much of my idea.

Dave responded first. "Well, Dean, that sounds . . . interesting. Yes, very interesting. How about you, Kamau? What kind of car will you make?"

Kamau twirled his block several times. "I'm really not sure how to make a car, but my dad is a carpenter. Maybe he can give me some ideas."

"I can help you," Dave said, sitting down on Kamau's bed. They chattered about what they were going to do with their cars. I took out my block of wood and tapped it absently in my palm. I'd have to come up with some great idea. I didn't have the patience to do detail work like Dave, so I had little chance of winning a special award for workmanship. I'd love to win the racing part, but my cars had always waddled along at tortoise speed. I'd never even come close to winning any speed awards. I remembered the year before when my car ran so poorly it barely made it to the end of the track. I'd blown on the wheels and poured oil on the nails that held the axles to the wheels. Nothing had helped. To make it even worse, in the last race, my front wheels finished the race before my car did.

Maybe this would be my year. My dad had told me to focus on my wheels. He said the wheels had more to do with speed than design, but I needed to think of some design. I still thought a banana was a pretty good idea, but if the other kids were going to laugh about it, I certainly wouldn't make a banana car.

After about half an hour, a nurse came in and herded us out. "Jon and Kamau need to rest," she said. We could tell she was happy that her patients were getting better.

We had hot dogs for supper. My little brother, Craig, took a big bite out of the middle of his and hit a chunk of cartilage. We often found pieces like that in the hot dogs sold in Kenya. Craig gagged, spit it out onto his plate, and jumped back from the table. "What is that?" he demanded. Dad explained what went into hot dogs and that sometimes certain parts like cartilage didn't get cut up well enough.

"I'm not eating that! Yuck!" Craig said and ran to his room. As I looked at his hot dog nestled in the bun with a large bite out of it, something clicked in my mind.

"Yes!" I said out loud.

"Yes, what?" my mom asked.

"Craig's hot dog there gives me a great idea for my Pinewood Derby car," I said. "I'm going to make my car look like a hot dog bun with a hot dog in it and one large bite taken out. I could paint the hot dog orange-red and paint yellow mustard and red ketchup on it."

"Sounds . . . different," my dad said.

"It has to be different to win the creativity prize," I said. "Remember the one last year that looked like a giant pencil? And the one that looked like the space shuttle?"

My dad agreed. "A hot dog shape should run fairly fast if you get your wheels fixed on straight. I know the rules say dads can't help with making your car, but I can give advice."

Craig poked his head around the corner. "Do I have to eat my hot dog?" he asked.

Mom had pity. "No, Craig. Come, I'll fix you a bowl of cereal."

"Can I have his hot dog?" I asked.

Mom raised her eyebrows. "You want to eat it?"

"No," I said. "I want to use it as my model for making my car."

She looked at me as I took a crinkled piece of only-used-once-

or-twice aluminum foil from the cupboard and wrapped up the hot dog and bun.

When Craig saw I wanted the hot dog he had rejected, he said, "I think I might want to eat my hot dog now."

"With that gross chunk of rubbery some-kind-of joint connection?" I asked.

"Dean!" my mother said sharply.

But my words had already had their desired effect. Craig's face paled. "Maybe I don't really want the hot dog," he said, turning away.

In my room later I took out my block of wood. Using Craig's unfinished hot dog as my model, I took my pencil and drew some lines along both sides of the block where I wanted the woodshop teacher to cut the wood using the band saw. Midway down the length of the block I drew in a jagged half-moon section that would look like a bite mark.

I held the block of wood and squinted at it, rotating it to see it from different angles. I got out my eraser and rubbed out one of the lines and carefully drew the line a bit higher. Satisfied with my work, I put the block in the plastic bag to take to school the next day. I wanted the woodshop teacher to cut it so I could get on with the job of further shaping and sanding. I got into bed to read my Bible. After reading chapter 3 of John, I stared at the plastic bag on my desk. The lines on the block of wood showed clearly through the plastic. What if the other Rhinos laughed at me for making a hot dog car? I decided not to take any chances. I got up and took the hot dog out of the aluminum foil and wrapped the foil around the block of wood. Feeling a bit hungry, I ate Craig's hot dog.

The next day after school we all ran to the woodshop. I stood in line with Matt and Dave. They showed me the lines they'd drawn on their blocks and described how great their cars would look. I glanced down at my block, glinting metallically in its aluminum foil wrapper. How would I get it cut without the other guys seeing my hot dog design? I remembered Jon. "I wonder if Jon drew his design yet?" I said out loud. "I heard he and Kamau both got out of the hospital today. Maybe I should run down to Jon's house and bring up his block to be cut if he's ready."

"Yeah, we should have thought of that earlier," Matt said. I could tell he didn't want to lose his place in line. Neither did Dave. They wanted to get on with the finish work of carving and sanding.

"You guys go ahead," I said. "I'm in no hurry to get my block cut. I'll run on down and get Jon's kit and have his and mine cut together. The woodshop is open until five-thirty."

I found Jon lying on the couch in his home. "My dad says I can go back to school tomorrow," he said. "I feel like I could go now, but he says I still need to rest. I hate resting. Look. The sun's shining, and it's beautiful outside."

I smiled. "I'm really glad you're feeling better. I came down to see if you had your design drawn on your wood for your Pinewood Derby car. I could take it up and get it cut on the band saw so you can go ahead with working on it. It might give you something to do the rest of today."

"Sounds good," said Jon, jumping off the couch and running into his bedroom. He brought out his block of wood with rough pencil marks along the side that would give his car an arrow-shaped front end and a squared off back. "It's not exactly like a Porsche 911," Jon said, "but it will do. I think it will be really fast. Look at that front end. It'll slice through the air."

I took both our blocks back up to the woodshop. Matt and

Dave were nowhere to be seen. They must have had their wood cut and have gone home to continue working.

The line was short so I wouldn't have to wait long. I didn't notice who was standing in line in front of me until Jill turned around. "Hi, Dean," she said with a big smile. "What's your car going to be this year?"

I felt my face turning hot and red.

CHAPTER TEN

THE HOT DOG CAR

"**H**ere's what I'm planning," Jill said, taking out her block of wood. "I thought I'd make a bathtub at first, but my dad told me I'd have to chisel out the inside of the tub. That sounded like a lot of work, so I decided to do this."

She pushed the piece of wood near my face. I looked at the pencil marks and smiled. "It looks great! What's it supposed to be?"

"You can't tell?" she asked, a frown wrinkling her normally pretty face.

"Well, it's pretty hard to tell what anything is going to look like just from the pencil marks. Why don't you describe it to me."

She smiled and said, "It's going to be a Maasai milk gourd. You know, those oblong ones that are shaped like a sausage. I'll have it cut in that type of shape and paint it brown. I even have permission from my mother to take the beautiful beaded stopper off a Maasai gourd she bought in the valley as a souvenir. I'll put that over the nose of the car so it will look authentic. And my dad suggested I tack a leather strap on the top."

"Sounds like a great idea," I said. "The only thing it will need is a smoky smell just like the inside of a real milk gourd. Have you ever drunk sour milk out of a Maasai milk gourd?"

She laughed. "I pretended to when we visited a Maasai *boma* near Suswa. I held the gourd to my mouth, but the smell almost made me gag, so I held it to my lips for a second before passing it on around the circle." She paused. "I wonder if I could make my car smell like smoke...." Her forehead wrinkled in concentration and a stray wisp of her straw-colored hair fell on her freckled cheek. She flicked the hair back into place with a toss of her head. "Thanks for the idea, Dean. You're great." Her words started a turmoil of excitement in my stomach.

"And what's your car going to look like this year?" Jill asked. "I can see it must be top secret. It's all wrapped in aluminum foil."

I looked around to be sure Matt and Dave weren't around. I whispered, "It's going to look like a hot dog."

"A hot rod?" Jill asked. "What kind of hot rod?"

"No, not a hot rod," I explained. "A hot dog."

I said this last part a bit too loudly. Rachel and Rebekah, who were in front of Jill, turned and stared at us. I tried to ignore them. I took out my pinewood block and showed it to Jill.

"That'll look really *safi*," she said. I could tell she really meant it.

Jill stepped forward to have her block cut. The whine of the saw and the spray of sawdust ended our conversation. I waved good-bye as she left the woodshop with Rachel and Rebekah. I handed both my block and Jon's to the woodshop teacher. I didn't bother to tell him whose was whose in case there might be any laughter over the hot dog idea. The teacher deftly sliced off the extra wood with the band saw. He had to make a number of small cuts to create the bite mark in the middle of my hot dog. I would have to go home and do a lot of chiseling to round off the ends, but the band saw sure gave me a big head start. I thanked him for his help and walked home, dropping off Jon's car on the way.

Over the next few weeks I worked on my car in the evenings. I chiseled out the ends of the wood so it looked like the hot dog was poking out of the bun. I whittled two lines along the length of the top of the piece of wood and rounded off the middle section to make it look like a hot dog in a bun. I sanded and sanded until I had worn chunks off my knuckles while getting the wood soft and smooth.

I wanted my car to be a surprise, so I painted it at home. I used a light brown paint for the hot dog bun, reddish-orange for the hot dog, and some yellow for the mustard. I also got a handful of sawdust from the woodshop. I dipped the sawdust in a small paint can lid filled with green paint. I scattered the green sawdust on top of the hot dog to look like relish. A bit of red paint made the final touch, a long line of ketchup down the length of the hot dog.

When I'd finished, I worked on the wheels. I spent Thursday evening before the competition adjusting the axles and attaching the wheels so they'd be straight and would run free. After each adjustment, I would hold the car in the air and spin each wheel. I went downstairs. "Hey, Dad, this wheel seems to be rubbing something. See how quickly it slows down." He turned the car upside down and pointed out where some excess paint clogged the wheel well. I carved the extra paint away.

After school the next day, Friday, we all had to register our finished cars for the race. First they would be weighed. The teachers had settled on a maximum weight. Any cars that weighed less as a result of cutting or chiseling off pieces of the block would be given a piece of lead to tack to the bottom of the car. Cars that weighed too much would have a hole drilled in the bottom to get it to the right weight. That way no one would have a weight advantage. After adding or subtracting the proper weight, the cars would be given a chance to run down the track that had been set up in the school assembly hall. Each entrant had to prove it could roll from the top of the track down to the bottom. After the test run, the cars would be set on a table by age-group. The judges would spend the rest of the afternoon deciding which cars were the best and runners-up in various categories.

I found Matt, Dave, and Jon, who had pretty much recovered from his frightening sickness. "Hey, there's Kamau," Dave said, pointing. "Come join us, Kamau."

Kamau worked his way over to us. He cradled his car, a replica of one of Kenya's overloaded, spring-sagging *matatus* or taxis. It had colorful streaks of paint and even a bumper sticker that read God is Able.

"Wow, your car looks great, Kamau," Dave commented. "I haven't seen it since I helped you draw the design. It even has a roof rack made out of twisted wire." Kamau smiled shyly.

As we stood in line, the others kept stroking their cars. Dave's looked immaculate. "It even has a Shell petrol advertisement and the driver's name along with the big number three," I said, congratulating him on his good work. I thought of my hot dog in the depths of my brown paper sack.

Dave and Kamau discussed how they'd built their cars. Matt and Jon spent so much time going on about the speed of their vehicles that no one asked what I'd designed.

I let all four of them go ahead of me. When it came my turn, I pulled my hot dog car out of the bag. I hadn't cut off as much wood as some of the others, so I only got a small flat piece of lead to bring my car up to maximum weight. Dave, standing in line for his test run, turned and saw me attaching the lead. "Is that your car, Dean?" he asked.

"Yeah," I answered, not too enthusiastically. I'd been dreading this moment. Now they'd all laugh at my car. I wished I'd made it look like a safari car. Or even like Matt's with at least a vaguely car-shaped body.

"Hey, that's *safi!*" Matt said when he saw my hot dog car. "I like that."

"Where'd you come up with the idea?" Dave asked. It was obvious he liked it, too.

"Well, it started when my little brother, Craig, gagged on his hot dog the day I got my kit."

Jon had a brief look at my car and nodded approvingly. "Is it fast? It's shaped kind of like a bullet. It should be fast." He turned to hand his car to the teacher standing on a ladder. The teacher placed Jon's car in the far lane against a movable starting block, which poked up through a hole in the bottom of the track. To start the race he'd turn a handle, the blocks in each lane would disappear like a trapdoor spider into its hole and the cars would all have an even start. Matt, Dave, and Kamau handed their cars over. I passed up my hot dog. Matt's and Jon's cars went the fastest. Kamau's wobbled, just like a real *matatu* on a potholed road. Mine was about the same speed as Dave's. We all picked our cars up at the bottom where they had stopped against a foam rubber pad at the end of the track. Matt and Jon were tickled with how fast their cars had gone.

Dave turned his upside down and studied it with narrowed eyes. He whipped out his red Swiss army knife and made some adjustments. He pushed his glasses to the end of his nose, held the car head-on at arm's length, and squinted. Another adjustment. Another examination. A grunt of satisfaction and he put his car on the table to await judging.

Dave's and Jon's were in the ten-year-old category. Kamau's and mine were for eleven-year-olds. Matt's stood defiant and ugly with the other cars done by twelve-year-olds.

"I'll see you guys this evening at the displays," I said, running home for supper.

Dave and I walked up together after supper and met the other three. We stood in line to see all the cars on the display tables. By now, the judges had made their decisions and small signs would be standing next to the winning cars. I could tell Dave was excited. He kept using his index finger to push his glasses back against his forehead. Matt and Dave weren't as concerned about winning any prizes for workmanship or creativity. They joined the Pinewood Derby to race cars down the track.

As the long line pythoned its way into the assembly hall, we could finally see the cars. From a distance it looked like a yellow card stood next to Dave's car. I whispered to him that he'd won something. Making a fist with his right hand, he pumped his arm up and down and whispered, "Yes!"

Suddenly I felt someone tugging on my arm. I looked up, startled. It was Jill. She had come back through the crowd and tugged at me. "Dean, we won!"

I followed, stumbling through the crowd as she dragged me to the table where our cars stood side by side. Her Maasai milk gourd and my hot dog had a yellow card in front reading, "Joint winners—Creative Design Award."

"Isn't that great, Dean!" Jill said jumping up and down. "We both won." Well, I must admit I was excited to have won a prize, but the way she carried on in front of everyone made me a bit nervous.

Everyone else in the line stopped and laughed, pointing at us. My face flushed hot. I looked back at the other Rhinos, expecting some support. Instead, Matt and Jon were mimicking Jill and pointing. Dave smiled, but it was a friendly smile.

"I . . . uh . . . I think it's great we both won, Jill. Your Maasai milk gourd looks pretty real. You did a good job, but I think . . . maybe I shouldn't have cut in front of the line like this."

I pulled away from her and went back to join the others. In her high spirits, Jill didn't seem to mind my abrupt departure.

"I didn't know you'd worked together with Jill," Matt teased. "Are you going to desert the Rhinos now that you've got a girlfriend?"

"She's not my girlfriend!" I hissed, looking around frantically, hoping no one had heard Matt. "And we didn't work together."

As the line inched ahead we passed Dave's car. The card next to it said he'd won first place for workmanship. We all pounded him on the back. I could see the healthy pride in his smile. He deserved the prize. I had hardly seen him since the kits had been handed out.

"Kamau, look!" Dave pointed at Kamau's *matatu*. "You won a prize for workmanship, too."

"My father will be proud of me," Kamau said, his eyes dancing.

As we passed by the table where Jill's car stood next to mine,

Jon frowned. "Something smells!" he announced, looking around. Even when hunting in the forest, Jon seemed to have a stronger sense of smell than the rest of us. He started sniffing and traced the smell to Jill's Maasai milk gourd. "It's this car of Jill's," he said. He sniffed again. "It really smells like a smoky, Maasai milk gourd!"

"Really?" I asked, leaning over. Jill's car gave off an acrid smell. "That was my idea. I wonder how she did it?"

"Your idea?" Matt asked, raising his left eyebrow. "I thought you said you didn't work together."

"We didn't work together. I just made a comment that it would be more authentic if it smelled like a real Maasai milk gourd."

"And when did you give her this comment?" Jon carried on the teasing. "At one of your planning sessions?"

"I happened to be standing in line next to her when we had our cars cut at the woodshop, and we talked for about one minute. We did not work together on our cars. I've hardly even seen her since then." I often looked at her in our classroom, but I wasn't about to tell the others that!

Dave cut in. "Lay off him, you guys. I think it's pretty cool that he won a prize for his hot dog car." He paused in front of the display of cars made by twelve-year-olds. "Hey, those two cars are great! One is a copy of the Sphinx from Egypt. The other is the Great Pyramid." He leaned over to inspect the two cars. "I wonder how they did it?"

The cars had won joint awards for creative design for their age-group. A giggle made Dave jump. "So you like our cars?" asked Rachel.

"Are those your cars?" Dave asked.

"Yes," answered Rachel. "You seem surprised. You didn't think girls could make decent Pinewood Derby cars?"

"No, that's not it. You did a great job."

Rebekah said, "Well, they don't run very fast down the track, but we had fun. And they won a prize."

We filed out of the building and went down to the school gym where the teachers had organized some games for us.

I woke up early the next morning, got some money from my parents, and ran up to school to buy doughnuts from the senior class. They ran a store on special days like field days and Pinewood Derby days so they could raise money for a trip at the end of the year called Senior Safari. They started selling doughnuts at 7 A.M. I bought a bag of one dozen and took them home so we could eat them for breakfast. I ate the first one as I walked down the path in the long shadows as the early morning sun filtered through the tall blue-gum trees.

After breakfast I went to Dave's house, and we walked up to the races. A crowd of people milled around the track. The woodshop teacher had built a racetrack especially for the cars. When all the pieces of the racetrack were set up, it filled one end of the school auditorium. The track started almost at ceiling level. The teachers would stand on ladders to put the cars in the starting area. Thin strips of wood divided the lanes and five cars could race at once. The track dropped off very steeply so the cars could gain speed before a gentle hump leading to the final straightaway.

We found Kamau and managed to get ourselves a good seat in the makeshift grandstand that had been built. Only the contestants whose cars were running in a race could stand next to the track. The rest of the time we had to watch from the grandstand.

The woodshop teacher tapped on a microphone as Jon and Matt crawled up over the back of the grandstand and joined us. After giving some general announcements about the day's schedule, the teacher cleared his throat and announced, "Let the Pinewood Derby begin!" Everyone clapped and cheered, and the first group of five racers, nine-year-olds, solemnly picked up their cars from the table and handed them to the starter for the first heat.

CHAPTER ELEVEN

RACING CARS

After about half an hour Jon and Dave raced their cars with the ten-year-olds. They had been assigned to different groups. Each group would have four races called heats. After each heat, the winner got four points, second place got three points, third place got two points, and fourth place got one point. Fifth place got no points. In Jon's first heat his car sailed down in first place. A number four went up next to Jon's name on the wooden scoreboard above the finish line. Any car earning ten points or more during the four heats would qualify for the finals in the afternoon. Jon's first place finish gave him a great start. His car finished first in the next two heats and third in the final heat, giving him fourteen points and allowing him to qualify for the finals. We cheered and whacked him on the back as he came back and sat with us.

Dave's group raced next. Dave looked seriously at his car and blew on the wheels before he handed it up to the starter. In the first race, Dave's Toyota finished third. Two points. Not very good. As he picked the car up from the finish line, we could see the flashing motion of his red knife as he bent over the car and made some changes to the wheel alignment. His car moved faster in the second race and he finished second. Three more points. He finished second by a nose in the third heat. In fact they had to do an instant replay of the finish three times to be sure Dave had actually gotten second. One of the teachers sat on a platform by the finish line and ran a video camera to settle any disputes. We enjoyed watching the instant replay on the TV screen after each close race. Dave now had eight points and one more race to go. In this race, it seemed like the rear end of Dave's car fishtailed a bit and slowed him down in the straightaway where another car flashed by just before the finish line. He had finished third, giving him a total of ten points—just enough to qualify. Dave had a worried look on his face as he walked over to the table and laid his car on its back and began tinkering with it again.

"I've got to get some more speed," he said when he joined us about ten minutes later. "I barely qualified. If I can't get my car to go faster I'm doomed in the finals."

When it came time for me to race, I found I'd been placed in a group with Jill and Kamau. "How did you get your car to smell like smoke?" I asked after we'd given our cars to the starter and stood at the finish line to await the result of the first heat.

"My mom let me splash liquid smoke on the car just before handing it in for judging," Jill answered.

"Liquid smoke? What's that?" I asked.

"The only smoke I know is the kind that fills my mother's kitchen and burns my eyes," put in Kamau.

"Liquid smoke comes in a bottle. My mom brings it out from the States and uses it on things like hamburgers to make them smell like they've been barbecued."

"All our food tastes smoky," commented Kamau. "Even our *chai*.

And we don't have to sprinkle smoke from a bottle." He shook his head, laughing.

"And they're off!" the announcer barked into the microphone.

Looking up at the cars from floor level was so different from in the stands. My wheels hadn't fallen off, and my hot dog rolled straight, but it couldn't keep up with Jill's Maasai milk gourd that shot like an arrow down the track. She won by over five feet. My hot dog came in a respectable second. Kamau's *matatu* came in last, but it did finish. Two other cars crashed on the way down. One had been going too fast and flipped upside down. The other lost its rear axle.

The owners made quick repairs, but the results were the same in all four heats. Jill came in first, qualifying with sixteen points. My car also qualified with twelve points from four second place finishes. I knew I wouldn't have much chance in the finals, but I still felt really good. I'd never finished as high as second in a Pinewood Derby race before. And I'd never qualified for the finals. I joined the other Rhinos with a big smile on my face.

I looked back and saw Kamau holding his matatu. "Come sit with us, Kamau," I called. "I'm sorry your matatu didn't win any races. At least you won a prize for workmanship." Kamau grinned.

"Aren't you going to work on your car to make it go faster?" Dave asked me.

"I don't know what else I can do," I said. "I worked for a long time on the wheels and I can't get them to spin any faster. I think it's just the design of the car. A hot dog just isn't too aerodynamic."

"Try racing it backward in the finals," Dave said. "It won't hurt and, who knows, maybe your car will go faster."

Matt swaggered over to get his car to race in the twelve-year-old heats. He'd won for the past two years and was confident he'd win again. "Come on, Matt," Jon yelled as the starter placed Matt's chunky block-of-wood-on-wheels on the track. Matt had stumbled on this design two years earlier. Since it had worked for two years, he hadn't made any changes. Just a gradual downhill cut for the front of the car with a square back untouched by anything but a few swabs of paint. Somehow the balance of weight on his design worked well.

Rachel and Rebekah's cars were in the same group. "I don't think Rachel and Rebekah have a chance against Matt," Dave said. We watched the cars drop off the starting blocks. Matt's made the downhill grade, but then it stopped dead in the track. "What's wrong with Matt's car?" Jon demanded. Though slow, Rachel and Rebekah's Egyptian history cars did reach the finish line.

Dave knew at once. "Something's hung up on the bottom," he said. "See, the wheels are still spinning like crazy, but it's not moving."

Matt had his hands together on top of his head. The stunned dismay on his face looked like my dog, Grump, when she'd suddenly been caught and tied up so she wouldn't follow me to school. Matt ran over and picked up his car.

"The nail holding the lead came loose," he said in a loud, complaining voice. He went to the table and one of the teachers helped him tack the lead on securely. In the second race, almost the same thing happened. This time, the lead stayed on, but the small nail to tack the lead on snagged on the track.

"Poor Matt," I said. "He can't qualify now."

Matt furiously ripped the lead off the bottom of his car and went to the table. This time they hammered the lead on the top of the car. His car looked as if it had been in a wreck with the fender littered on top, but his car was fast! It came in first on the last two heats, but the eight points for two first place finishes wasn't enough to qualify for the finals.

"Man, what a rip-off!" Matt said as he slammed into his seat.

None of us answered. We knew how he felt.

"To lose two races because of the lead!" Matt went on. "It wouldn't have been so bad if my car was slow. But did you see those last two races? I had the fastest car on the track, and I'd have won first place in the finals for sure."

"Maybe you should have checked how the lead was put on," Dave said, gently.

"You've got all the answers, don't you, Mr. Perfect Craftsman?" Matt said sharply. Dave's shoulders sagged. "Okay, okay." Matt looked sheepish. "I'm sure you're right. You always are. I just don't have time to take care of details like that. Did you see how fast my car went? Man, I could have won."

As the races went on, Matt got bored. He no longer had a car in the running so he suggested we go out and play. Since the finals didn't start until 2 P.M. we agreed. We bought hamburgers and Cokes from the seniors. As we sat under a cedar tree, Jill, Rachel, and Rebekah came up.

"Sorry about your car, Matt," Jill said.

Matt had to impress the girls. "Ah, it was no big deal," he said. I raised my eyebrows to hear that! "But my car did go fast when I got it fixed, didn't it?" Matt asked, trying to salvage some of his battered pride.

"It was fast, all right," Jill said. "Well, good luck in your races, Jon . . . Dave . . . Dean," she looked at each of us in turn and smiled.

"Thanks," Dave said.

"Yeah," Jon agreed. "And I really liked the smell of your car, Jill. Just like a real Maasai milk gourd."

"That was a great idea," Matt said, nodding.

Jill smiled at me, "Actually, it was Dean who gave me the idea."

The guys all looked at me again with knowing grins. "You sure you didn't work together, Dean?" Matt asked.

"You're the one who figured out how to do it, Jill," I said "Tell them about the liquid smoke."

The other Rhinos became fascinated with the fact that some company sold smoke in a bottle and after Jill and her friends left, they talked about that and didn't tease me about liking Jill.

Matt wasn't too excited about watching the finals, but we persuaded him. "We watched you last year even though none of us qualified," said Dave. "Remember?"

Reluctantly, Matt joined us.

Jon and Dave joined three others in the ten-year-old final. Despite all of Dave's loving care and adjustments, he couldn't get his car going fast enough to win. Jon's car never slowed down. It sped down the track, giving no one else a hope. Somehow Jon had gotten the combination just right: wheels, weight, design. Dave finished a respectable second. He shook Jon's hand after the race. The Rugendo Rhinos had taken first and second place.

My race was next. During the lunch break Dave had used the saw blade of his knife and helped me to file back a section of the car's body near the front wheel to see if it would run faster. In the first race Jill's car rocketed ahead to win. I finished a distant third. Dave whistled to get my attention and made a twisting motion with his hands. He wanted me to race the car backward. I sighed.

Why not? I handed the car up and said I wanted it to be turned around. The teacher complied. To my surprise my car really motored. I came in second to Jill in the second race. I ran back to the starter with my car. "Race it backward again," I said. This time Jill's car was in lane four, which had been the slowest lane during the day. The race was close and in the replay it showed that I'd won. I leaped in the air. After three races I had nine points. Jill had eleven points. Everything rested on the last race.

We gave our cars to the starter and ran to the finish line to watch. I can still see the final race as if in slow motion. The starting blocks dropped. The cars plummeted down the steepest part of the track. Down, down, then up over the gentle hump. The beaded cap of Jill's milk gourd crested the small hump first. The cars whizzed down the straightaway. My hot dog was even with Jill's milk gourd. Then it fell away. Half an inch. Then one inch. I wanted to reach over and push my car faster. Shouts erupted. The race was over. Jill had won by the length of the beaded leather stopper on the nose of her car.

I choked back the emotions that wanted to bubble out. I blinked back the tears. I picked up my car and congratulated Jill.

The others comforted me. "You did great, Dean," Matt said. "Too bad you didn't run your car backward in all the races. Still, not a bad haul for the Rhinos this year. Jon got a first for racing. Dave and Dean, you both got a second prize in the races and trophies for workmanship and creativity. And Kamau, you won a prize for workmanship as well. We'll have to look into making you an official member of the Rugendo Rhinos. It looks like I'm the only one who didn't win anything this year." He sighed. "That's OK. I'll still cheer for you guys when you get your awards at the ceremony tonight."

We stayed and watched the older kids and the staff members race. Kamau ran home to show his dad the prize he'd won.

When I got home in the late afternoon, I could hear voices. Some Kenyans stood near the door. I recognized Kamau. "Kamau, *Ni atia?*" I said, asking, "What's up," in Kikuyu.

"When I got home I found that one of our cows had died mysteriously," Kamau said, "and my parents think it has something to do with the curse that Ngugi's father has put on my family. We've come with Pastor Waweru to get your father. The *wazee,* the church elders, think we need to have a confrontation against the demonic forces and end this attack."

MYSTERIOUS BONES

I went into our house and found my father talking with Pastor Waweru. They agreed to go to Ngugi's father as a group of elders. They said they would plan on going the next day, Sunday, in the afternoon. That would give time for each of the elders to pray and ask for God's protection and direction in the meeting.

As Pastor Waweru left with Kamau's family, I asked my dad why they had to go pray again. "Didn't the first prayer work when Jon and Kamau got better? Wasn't that the end of the spiritual battle?"

"The battle goes on all the time, Dean," my dad answered. "We did win a big victory when Jon and Kamau were sick and God healed them, but apparently, things aren't yet settled for Ngugi's father. He is still angry and is bringing on more trouble for Kamau's family. We have to get to the root of it."

"Well, I'll pray for you."

"Thanks, Dean, I'll be praying about this, too. Hey, I saw your car come in second place in the race today. You did well."

"Yeah, that's the closest I've ever come to winning in the race. Thanks, Dad, for your advice about the wheels. Are you going to come see me get my award at the ceremony tonight?"

"I wouldn't miss it, Dean," he said. "Mom and I will both be there. And I'll bring my camera and get some pictures."

The next day Dad didn't come home after church. Mom said he and the other church elders had decided to fast and pray before going to Ngugi's father. So we ate Sunday dinner without him. We prayed for all the men and later during the afternoon I stopped several times to pray for Dad and the church elders.

Dad came home in the evening and as we sat in our living room dominated by a beautiful zebra skin on the wall, I asked him what had happened.

"We prayed before going to Ngugi's father's home," my dad began. "We didn't accuse him of having a part in the mysterious death of the cow, but we asked him why he had called the witch doctor. Ngugi's father was hostile from the start, and demanded we all leave. Pastor Waweru held firm, asking the others to pray and, in the name of Jesus, we bound any power of the spirits over that place until they got an answer."

I shivered. "Doesn't this battle ever end?" I asked.

"Not until heaven," my dad answered. "Anyway, Ngugi's father finally calmed down and explained how he had visited a witch doctor in the nearby town after Ngugi died. The witch doctor told him Ngugi's death was caused by angry spirits. After Kamau's grandfather accepted Christianity, the family no longer poured out offerings to the spirits of their ancestors. The ancestral spirits were angry, but because of the strength of Kamau's grandfather's faith in Christ, they had been able to do nothing. Nor could they harm Kamau's father. According to the witch doctor, the spirits felt they could attack Kamau."

"Why Kamau?" I asked.

"I'm not sure," my dad said. "Maybe they believe he's vulnerable because he's young. According to the witch doctor, since Ngugi was with Kamau on the day of the spiritual attack, they both got sick. Ngugi died while Kamau survived. On hearing this, Ngugi's father asked the witch doctor to help him get revenge for Ngugi's death. That's when Kamau and Jon became so sick. When our prayers stopped that, Ngugi's father had the witch doctor bring a curse on Kamau's family's cattle. He said one cow is dead. The rest will follow. Kamau's father's eyes gaped at that. He only owns five cattle, but they are his savings account for the future of his children. Without cattle, he will have nothing to help Kamau pay the bride price to get married."

I edged forward on the couch. "What happened then?" I asked.

"Well, we prayed," Dad answered. "It was powerful to see the strong prayers of faith of the church elders and Pastor Waweru as they stood against this attack of Satan. By the time we had all finished, Ngugi's father was subdued. Quiet. But not finished. I don't think that man is finished."

"What happens next?" I asked. A strong gust of wind swept by the house and branches from a big cedar tree scraped loudly against the roof.

"Well, we have to keep praying. As long as Kamau and his family keep their spiritual guard up, Jesus is more powerful than Satan and his demons. We know that. We've seen it, but if they let their guard down . . ."

"How?" I asked.

"Letting sin go unconfessed. Forgetting to keep their prayer shield up. I don't know all the ways. Things are under control now, but we need to keep praying."

Craig popped his head out of the door to the bathroom, red as the snail in a bull mouth helmet shell. He had a towel wrapped around his waist and was dripping dry. Dad pulled Craig onto his lap and we read from the Bible and prayed for Kamau and his family.

"I wish there was some way for Ngugi's father to stop being mad at Kamau's family," I said after our prayer time.

"That would end things," Dad agreed, "but he was still very angry today. We'll have to keep praying that God will change his heart."

As I walked to school with Matt, Jon, and Dave the next morning, I was still thinking about Ngugi's death and all the things that had come about since then. "What are you thinking about?" Jon teased. "Jill?"

"No, not her." I explained what had gone on the day before. "I know that when you and Kamau were so sick it was some sort of demonic attack. But what about the first sickness? The one where Ngugi died and Kamau was so sick. I know the witch doctor says the spirits caused it, but . . . I don't know. What if it was caused by something else? If we could find out and prove it, Ngugi's dad would stop being angry and would stop bringing more curses on Kamau's family."

"I'm in the mood for a hike in the woods after school today," Matt said. "Why don't we go back to the place where we found Ngugi and Kamau? Maybe we'll find some clue."

The others were enthused. My face mirrored the fear I felt. I think I looked a bit like an ugly gray tilapia fish from Lake Naivasha. Matt frowned. "What's the matter, Dean? Don't you want to go? It was your idea!"

"I . . . I guess I'm just remembering the last time we went there." I told Matt and Jon how Dave and I had gone back to get tadpoles at the end of the day Ngugi died and about the shadowy movement we'd seen.

"Or thought we saw," Dave admitted. "I don't know what it was, but it seemed spooky. I'm not sure I want to go back."

"I'm not sure I want to go there either," Matt said, "but that's the place we'll have to start searching. We'll have to go if we're going to uncover any clues. Unless you don't want to go at all."

"I agree, we should go," I said, "but what if I'm wrong? What if the first sickness was caused by demons, too? Would we be in danger by going back there?"

We walked in silence. Suddenly Jill joined us. "What's going on?" she asked. "Usually you guys come past my house talking like crazy."

Matt told her what we'd been talking about.

"Why don't you pray? Ask God to protect you if there are any unclean spirits at the place. And pray for help to find any clues if the sickness had some other cause," she said.

Why hadn't we thought of that? "Yeah," Matt said. "We could pray."

"When are you going?" Jill asked.

"After school," Matt answered.

"I'll come," Jill said.

"I don't think so," said Matt. "It might be scary or something."

"Try to stop me," Jill said. She turned, waved, and ran off.

"Great," Matt said, "now we've got your girlfriend coming along."

"She is not my girlfriend!" I said firmly. "How many times do I have to say that?"

We agreed to meet at Matt's house after school so we could try to sneak away without Jill following us, but as we started down the path, she stepped out from behind a bush and said, "Hi, guys." She fell in line behind Dave who brought up the rear.

Matt gave an exasperated shrug of his shoulders and led the way. As we came within sight of the pond, Matt slowed down. "Maybe this is a good time to pray," he said.

We quietly asked God to keep us safe and to help us solve the mystery of Ngugi's death. Silently we approached the area where we'd found Kamau and Ngugi lying on the ground. "Fan out and look for anything that might be useful," Matt said. Jill stayed close to me. I went behind a short but very bushy green tree that shaded the area. Gray-feathered birds hopped in the tree, nibbling at the red berries that clustered at the ends of the branches. We called the birds yellow bums because of the lemon-yellow patch of feathers under their tails. My dad said their proper name was yellow-vented bulbuls. The yellow bums flapped wildly away as we walked near the tree. I got down on one knee and looked around. "I don't see anything," I said.

"Neither do I," Jill answered, who had been sifting dirt through her fingers. Dave came back from searching by the edge of the pond. He shook his head.

Matt and Jon dug around the blackened place in the grass where the two boys had built their fire. Jon picked up a few things and set them in a pile in the grass. "What have you guys found?" I asked.

"We're not sure," Matt answered. "Jon has found some slender bones. They're almost like chicken bones."

"Chicken bones?" Dave asked. "Don't witch doctors often sacrifice chickens when contacting spirits?"

I felt imaginary creepy crawlies all over my back.

"Maybe," Jon said, "but I think this has nothing to do with the witch doctor. You see this partially burned stick here? It looks like the kind we would use to roast hot dogs on a fire. My guess is that Kamau and Ngugi ate some kind of meat. Cooked it over their fire. And maybe the meat was bad. I don't know. Maybe they found someone's dead chicken, and it had died of some sort of disease."

"That could be," Matt said. "I've heard that if an animal dies of some sickness that sounds like 'ants' something or other—"

"Anthrax," said Jill.

"That's right, anthrax," finished Matt. He frowned at Jill for knowing the name of the disease before him. "Anyway, I've heard that if an animal dies of anthrax and anyone eats the meat, they get really sick. It could be something like that."

Jill leaned over. "Look at this bone over here," she said pointing to a place several yards away. "There's something dry stuck to it. It might be sinew or something."

"Let's take it to the hospital," Jon said. "Maybe my dad can test the bones or the sinew at the laboratory to see if the animal had some sort of disease."

"And we can ask Kamau what they ate," I said. "That might give us a clue as well."

"Solving mysteries isn't as hard as I thought," Jill whispered to me as we headed back to Rugendo. "Maybe we girls should form our own club."

I was glad Matt, leading the way as usual, hadn't heard what Jill said.

THE DOROBO HUNTER

We ran up to the hospital. Jon went in and tracked down his dad and told him what we'd found. Dr. Freedman came out and talked to all of us for a few minutes. "I'll take these bones and we'll see what they can find in our lab. I doubt they'll be able to discover anything useful. The bones are kind of dried out, but maybe some bacteria will show up. Maybe anthrax, maybe something else. We'll have the lab check and see what shows up under the microscope. I don't think these are chicken bones, though. I wonder what they are?"

"Let's go ask Kamau," I said.

We left Dr. Freedman and headed for Kamau's house. He lived on the other side of a small stream where the mission station drew its water. The mission houses had all been built originally on a flat area where nobody had been living. Over the years, many Kenyans had moved from nearby villages to live right next to the compound. Some families came many years before to go to school or to find work. Others had gravitated down from villages further up in the hills as families grew and plots of land could no longer be divided for each of the adult sons. A sizable new town had grown up on the other side of the river with shops, and *chai* houses, as well as homes and small farms.

"Who knows which house is Kamau's?" asked Matt.

"I do," said Dave. "His dad works with my dad. Sometimes my dad gives him a ride home after work. It's not too far."

At Kamau's, a sheep stood tethered to a stake. It ripped up shiny green grass and looked at us silently. Kamau came out from the cookhouse carrying an empty plastic jug. Once a white oil container, the jug was now a dirty brown. He greeted us. "I was just going down to the river to fetch water," he said.

We offered to help. He gave us each a one-gallon jug, and we walked down the steep path. "We've been wondering," Matt began, "if you and Ngugi ate any meat the day you got sick. Like a chicken or something."

"Why do you ask?" Kamau looked at us curiously.

"Well, we found some bones at the spot where we discovered you and Ngugi," Matt went on. "We thought maybe it had come from a sick bird or animal and you'd gotten sick from the meat."

"You don't think our sickness that day was caused by the spirits?" he asked.

"We're not sure," I said. "When both you and Jon almost died, we know that sickness was caused by evil spirits, but what if the first sickness wasn't caused by spirits? We could show Ngugi's father, and he'd stop having the witch doctor put curses on you and your family."

We reached the river and held the jugs under the water to let them fill up.

"Maybe you're right," Kamau said, "but I know the meat wasn't bad. It was a rabbit. Ngugi and I killed it with a club that morning. It was very healthy. And the meat was sweet. No, I don't think it could have been the meat. I still don't know. I think it was the spirits that made us get sick."

We hauled the water back up to Kamau's house, thanked him for his help, and left. "Well, we know what kind of meat it was," Matt said. "Rabbit."

We went back to the hospital. Dr. Freedman told us they wouldn't have results on the test until the next day. The shadows had lengthened. We said good-bye and headed for home. I walked Jill partway to her house.

"Well, bye," I said. "Thanks for helping us search for the bones. You're a good looker."

"Why, thanks for the compliment," Jill responded. "Do you really think I look good?"

Thankfully the evening shadows hid my blush. "I meant you're good at looking for things. You found those bones, remember."

"Oh, so you don't think I'm good-looking?"

"You are," I fumbled for words. "I was talking about something else, but yes, you are, uh, cute."

"I guess that's a compliment," Jill said. A smile tugged the edges of her lips upward as she walked up her driveway.

The next day after lunch while Matt and I kicked a soccer ball around the field, Jon and Dave came and joined us. "My dad said the lab finished examining the bones," said Jon. "The results were negative. They couldn't find anything that would have made Kamau and Ngugi sick. No bacteria or poison in the bones and sinew. Nothing at all."

The first bell rang for school. "We need to decide what to do next," Matt said. "Let's meet at our clubhouse in the *mugumo* tree at four o'clock. That will give me enough time to go home after school and have a snack."

"Hey, what are you guys planning?" Jill interrupted as she walked over with Rebekah and Rachel. "Did you find out anything about the bones I found?"

Jon answered, "They had no trace of anything harmful."

"So what do we do next?" asked Jill.

Matt shrugged. "We're not sure," he said.

"Well, if you Rhinos aren't going to unravel this mystery, we girls will. Won't we?" Jill asked Rachel and Rebekah, who nodded and followed her toward the classrooms.

Matt's eyes squinted with anger as he hissed at me, "Dean, don't you dare tell Jill where we're going after school. We don't want her tagging along. We've got to solve this mystery before she butts in again."

We gathered at our tree fort and discussed everything we knew. "Well," Matt concluded, "it doesn't look like we've made any progress in finding some physical cause for Ngugi's death. Maybe it was a spiritual attack from Satan."

Jon sat up, suddenly alert. He moved to one of the small windows we had cut out of the wall. "Look down there!" he whispered. We all crowded by the window.

A small brown man crouched, partially hidden behind a bush. He peered ahead into the ravine below. Then, like an escaped shadow, he slipped away from his hiding place. We could see he wore a brown cloth tied toga-style over his shoulder. A large knife in a leather sheath was strapped to his waist. A wooden quiver of arrows hung on a leather strap over his back. And he carried a bow. He eased his way forward, an arrow strung and ready for instant release.

"Hey, who are you and what are you doing?" shouted Matt in Kikuyu.

In that instant a thrashing sound filled the ravine and a bushbuck exploded out of the thick brush, sprinting for safety. The small man looked up to see who had interrupted his hunt. He shook his bow angrily at us and then disappeared, melting into the shadows of the forest.

"That guy was different," Matt said.

"I wish you hadn't shouted," Jon said. "I would have liked to see if he could hit that bushbuck. Man, how did he even know the bushbuck was there? I didn't see a thing."

Matt defended himself. "I couldn't see any bushbuck either. For all I knew he might have been planning to shoot a person. So I called out."

"Maybe we can learn something by looking around," Jon said.

We clambered down out of our tree fort, but not even Jon's tracking skills could find anything about the mysterious little hunter. We went home, not sure what to do next besides continue to pray for Kamau's family.

That night I asked my dad about the hunter we'd seen in the forest. He listened with interest and started nodding. "He was probably a Dorobo," Dad said.

"What's a Dorobo?" I asked.

"Well," he explained, "they are a small tribe that lives by hunting and collecting honey in the forests. I've only met a few, but small groups of them live in most of the thick forest areas of Kenya."

"Can you tell me more?" I asked. I liked collecting knowledge about the different tribes that lived in Africa.

"From what I've gathered, they lived in Kenya before all of the larger tribes moved in. As the Maasai, Kikuyu, and Kalenjin moved into this area in a big migration from the north, they gradually displaced the Dorobo. Actually, the more proper name for the tribe is Okiek, but most people call them Dorobo, which comes from the Maasai word for the tribe, *Iltorrobo*, meaning 'poor people' or 'people without cows.'"

"Why have we never seen any before if they live in our forest?" I asked.

"Well, the Dorobo are famed for being very reclusive and se- cretive," my dad answered. "But somehow I doubt there's a group living in our forest or I'm sure we'd have heard about them. Our forest isn't that large, you know. Just the three or four miles be- tween here and the plains. The man you saw might just be passing through, looking for some animals to hunt. Actually, the Dorobo did live near here years ago. The Kikuyu called them the Athi, the pioneers. As the Kikuyu moved in and started farming, the Dorobo traded vast tracts of forestland for beehives."

"They did what?"

My dad laughed. "Traded their forest for beehives. You see, the Dorobo love honey more than anything. They love to eat it raw, right from the honeycomb. Until the Kikuyu arrived, the Dorobo had to search hard to find honey in trees with holes or in small cracks in rock cliffs. They would follow a bird called the honey guide, which showed them where honey was in return for a share in the honey. Or they'd follow the bees themselves, but it was a pretty haphazard business. Then they found the Kikuyu had in- vented portable beehives by splitting logs in two. They hollowed out the middle of a three-foot section and tied the two halves back together using vines. They could dangle the log beehive from any tree they wanted and come back and check it from time to time to see if they had any bees coming in to make honey."

"So the Dorobo traded their land for beehives," I finished.

"Yes. In those days there was plenty of forest and the Dorobo ranged from place to place anyway. So they didn't think they were giving up much. And in exchange, they got beehives and could find honey with a lot less effort."

"I guess it was a good trade," I said.

"Until recently," my dad said. "With the surging population here in Kenya, the agricultural tribes like the Kikuyu and Kipsigis have cut down a lot of the forest for farmland. So the Dorobo that remain are being pushed further and further into the remaining forest area."

"How do you know all this stuff?" I asked.

"I've done some study with Mr. Njogu, the Kenyan editor at our magazine. We did a series on different tribes as well as some recent articles on the effects of Kenya's birthrate, which was the world's highest until a few years ago."

All the talk about Dorobo and hunting reminded me about our genet cat trap. With all our excitement about the spiritual warfare and the Pinewood Derby, we hadn't been checking it regularly. I decided I would wake up early the next morning and have a look.

My alarm clock woke me in the usual way, clanking until I hammered the button down. I turned on my light to see what time it was—6 A.M. I yawned, got up, and dressed, dragging an old sweatshirt on over my school clothes to ward off the damp, early-morning cold.

I looked around in the kitchen for some new bait for the trap.

My dad hadn't been fishing recently so I had no fish heads. I finally grabbed a piece of bread and stuck it in my pocket. At the door I put on an old pair of boots. With all the dew on the grass and bushes, it would be wet and I didn't want to ruin my new tennis shoes. Even though they were new—less than a month old—my tennis shoes already had an orange-brown tint to them. It was impossible to keep white shoes white with all the dirt around Rugendo, but if I could avoid getting them wet, they would last longer.

I slid down parts of the trail as I hurried to the place where we'd set the trap. The soft rattling burp of colobus monkeys echoed through the ravines. I slowed down to catch my breath when suddenly a big brown francolin scudded out from behind a bush, flapping and screeching like a maniac. The bird had a habit of doing that. Even the Kikuyu people had a special name for the francolin, meaning the bird that makes even grown men scared. My heart thumped like the machinegun mode on an electronic keyboard.

I finally arrived at the tree where we'd hidden our trap. Reaching down carefully, I pushed aside the bushes. The trap was still set. Nothing had disturbed it and the peanut butter on the stick had turned gray with mold. I tried to attach the piece of bread to the stick. I really didn't want to touch the moldy peanut butter so I laid the bread on the stick and gave it a squeeze with my hand. The bread stuck, forming an outer layer around the peanut butter. I pushed the box trap back into its hiding place. I'd report my findings to the other guys and we'd have to put some proper bait in the trap.

As I stood up I glimpsed a flicker of motion to my right.

HUNTING WITH POISON ARROWS

I almost leaped out of my boots. The small brown man with the bow and arrow slipped out from behind a tree. My throat was too dry to scream. I wanted to run, but my legs felt heavier than when I finished playing soccer on a wet, red-clay field and had huge clumps of mud clinging to my shoes.

The man smiled. I felt myself take a breath, but I looked around warily, hoping he'd leave so I could escape. Instead he motioned at the bush where I'd just hidden the trap. I looked down slowly at the bush and then back to the little man. I pointed at the bush with a frown on my face. He nodded and squatted down, pointing again.

I tried some Swahili. *"Unataka nini?"* I asked. "What do you want?"

"Kuona mtego," he answered in Swahili. At least we could communicate a little bit, but I didn't know Swahili too well. He had said he wanted to see something. I didn't know what the word

mtego meant, but I assumed it must mean our trap. So I reached under the bush and dragged it out.

In an instant the man had crouched down and gingerly touched the trap. He felt around the corners, pouting out his lips and nodding seriously. Putting his head upside down like a flamingo dredging for food, he peered into the box. Seeing the bait stick he reached in and tugged on it. The door promptly fell on his arm. He jumped back, pulling his arm out of the box. He examined the wires and the pulley that let the door drop down to trap an animal inside. He gave an approving grunt. Bending over again, he lifted the door and unwired the bait stick. He stood up, holding the stick covered with the moldy peanut butter and the piece of bread crumpled around it. He sniffed it. He wrinkled his nose up and grimaced. He said some words I didn't understand and flung the stick into the woods in obvious disgust.

"Yeah, it smells kind of bad," I muttered. "No wonder we didn't catch anything in our trap."

He looked at me questioningly. I tried to explain in Swahili but failed.

The man stepped behind the tree. I thought he would disappear again, but he popped back again holding the limp body of a dead blue monkey.

"*Tumpili,*" he said, giving me the Swahili name for the monkey. He pulled out his knife, almost a small sword, that he carried in a leather sheath tied to a rawhide thong around his waist. The knife had been honed razor sharp and the blade almost measured a foot in length. He swung it at a nearby bush, lopping off a branch with one swing. I cringed.

Taking the branch, he stripped off the bark and cut a stick about the same size as the bait stick he'd thrown away. After sharpening the stick, he turned to the monkey where he'd laid it on the ground, and with a few deft strokes of his knife he cut off a small strip of monkey meat. He stabbed the sharp end of the stick through the meat and wrapped the meat around the stick several times, tying it like a shoelace.

Dropping to his knees, he reached into our trap and attached the new bait stick to the trip wire. I showed him how to set the door of the trap. He pushed the box back under the bush. Using the dead monkey as a broom he swept over the area leading to the trap. Draping the monkey over his shoulder, he motioned for me to move away. I followed him up the path. He stopped and pointed back at the trap and told me in Swahili that we would catch something by the next morning.

I thanked him and asked him if he was a Dorobo. *"Ndiyo,"* he answered, "it is so."

I told him I had learned from my dad how his people were famous hunters. The man smiled.

"Can you show me and my friends how you hunt?" I asked. He agreed to meet us after school at our tree fort. "The place where we interrupted your hunt yesterday," I said. "Do you know time? Can you be there at 4 P.M.?"

He lifted up his arm to display a digital watch. He told me he'd traded some honey for the watch at the market.

I told him I had to go to school and we'd meet later. He held out his hand in farewell and told me his name. "I am Kosen," he said.

"And I'm Dean," I responded. We shook hands briefly. I started up the hill. When I turned to wave good-bye, he had already slipped into the forest. I ran most of the way back home, stopping only twice because I had a side ache. At the house I tore off my boots, and grabbed a piece of toast to eat on the way to school.

"Did you catch anything in your trap?" my dad asked.

"No," I answered, "but we will tomorrow."

He raised his eyebrows and set his coffee cup down. "What makes you so sure?" he asked.

"Remember that Dorobo guy we saw in the forest yesterday? Well, this morning he met me at the trap and helped me to set it with a piece of monkey meat for bait. And this afternoon he's agreed to take us hunting and show us how he tracks animals and things. I can't wait to tell the other Rhinos."

"Sounds like fun," my dad said. "I'd sure enjoy coming along, but I'm going to Nairobi today to interview a pastor who grew up in a home with two mothers."

"Two mothers?" I asked, my question spilling out around the peanut butter and jam toast I had just stuffed into my mouth.

"We're doing a magazine on polygamy," he explained. "That's when a man marries more than one wife. To get the inside look on how polygamy affects family members, we're interviewing this pastor who grew up in a polygamous home. Anyway, when I get back tonight I want you to tell me how the hunting trip went."

I waved good-bye and hurried out the door. In the distance I could hear the first bell ringing at school. If I ran, I could just get there before the second bell rang in five minutes.

At recess I went to the water fountain first. The peanut butter had left a stale taste in my mouth. Since I'd eaten most of it running up the hill, I hadn't had a chance to brush my teeth. Drawing in large gulps of water, I squirted it around in my mouth trying to clean my mouth out. I spit the water out on the nearby banana plant before taking another drink of water.

I went looking for Matt. I found him on the soccer field. He'd already appointed teams and told me to join his team. As the players argued about who would play where, I told Matt about the Dorobo man being willing to take us hunting after school. Matt was so excited he couldn't concentrate on the soccer game and fluffed two easy chances to score.

We all met at Matt's after school and jogged down to our tree fort together. We looked around when we got there but couldn't see Kosen, the Dorobo hunter, anywhere. Matt blamed me right away. "I hope you didn't get things messed up, Dean," he said. "Maybe when you were talking to him in Swahili you mixed up the day or the time. Or maybe he said he wouldn't come and you thought he meant he would come."

"I'm sure he said he'd meet us here today at four. But I don't know. Sometimes I mix things up in Swahili, especially the times. You know how Africans start counting the hours at the beginning of the day so seven in the morning is *saa moja* or the first hour. I'm pretty sure I told him we'd meet at the tenth hour and that's four o'clock, isn't it?"

"We also have to remember that this is Africa," Dave said. "Even if the guy did agree to meet us at this time, he may be late. Judging by the weddings I've gone to with my parents that are scheduled for ten in the morning and start in the late afternoon, he could be very late."

We heard a snort of laughter and Kosen appeared. He'd been standing next to a tree about ten yards away, but until he laughed we hadn't seen him. With his soft brown blanket and his coppertone skin he blended into the background.

"*Twende.* Let's go," he said in greeting and strode into the forest. We followed him without saying a word, Jon right on his heels. I let Dave and Matt go ahead of me. Even when we Rhinos stalked pigeons, Jon and Matt always chided me for making too much noise. I didn't want to annoy the Dorobo hunter today. I tried to pick my way carefully through the bushes and the dead branches on the ground, determined not to make any noise. I kept my eyes focused on the path in front of me. That's why I didn't notice the others had already stopped until I bumped into Dave who had hunkered down in a baseball catcher's position to watch. After I bumped him, he teetered and almost fell over, but caught his balance with one hand. His face told me he didn't appreciate my bump. I started to say I was sorry when Matt turned and drew a line through his neck with his index finger in a silencing gesture. I crouched like the others and watched Kosen. His shoulders leaned forward slightly and he stood absolutely still, peering into the forest. I tried to follow his gaze, but I could only see rippling shadows of dark and darker under the thick canopy of trees. After a few minutes that seemed to last for an hour, he signaled for us to follow. He made no sound as he eased forward. Unlike me, Kosen didn't pay any attention to where he stepped. He looked ahead. As he stepped, his feet seemed to touch the ground and gently draw up as if on a cushion. He glided ahead of us. I let Dave get several steps ahead of me before following.

Our line came to a halt again after another five minutes. The Dorobo motioned us to join him. He pointed to the ground and said in Swahili, "A large bushbuck passed by here about two minutes ago."

Matt translated for us, before asking, "How can you tell?"

Kosen said, "The shape of the print shows me it was a bush-buck, not some other animal. The depth of the print in the ground tells me how heavy the animal is. And I smelled the blade of grass that had been stepped on. It still emitted a certain scent, telling me the animal had passed by within the past two minutes."

Jon squatted down and peered, nodding excitedly. I was still trying to see the footprint in the dead leaves.

We worked our way through the thickly forested area for another ten minutes and arrived at the edge of a small clearing. Kosen had his bow ready by the time I knelt down next to the others. He had already lined the arrow up on the taut bowstring. Ever so slightly he drew the bowstring back, gripping the shabby-looking feathers on the end of his arrow. I couldn't even see what he was aiming at, but we all held our breath and watched. The bow bent as the string stretched. He held that position momentarily before releasing the arrow. A soft whirring hum whispered as the arrow disappeared. At almost the same instant a bushbuck gave a startled bark and leaped out from where he'd been browsing across the glade. The arrow had struck the animal in the shoulder, but as the buck rushed away, the arrow fell out. With a big smile, Kosen ran into the clearing and picked up his arrow.

"Looks like he didn't get much power into his shot," Matt said. "It was a fun stalk, but I'm a bit disappointed. I thought he'd kill the animal."

Kosen picked up the arrow and very carefully wrapped the metal arrowhead with a long strip of softened leather. He made wide loops around the arrowhead, being very careful not to touch it. The arrowhead, shaped like a small knife blade, had no barbs.

Matt asked him why he was wrapping the arrow so carefully.

Kosen said one word. "*Sumu.*" It meant 'poison.'

"You used a poison arrow?" Matt asked.

The man nodded and placed the now-wrapped arrow back in his quiver. He bent over and found a spot of red liquid in the grass.

"*Damu,*" he said. Blood. And he started following the trail. Within a hundred yards we found the dead bushbuck.

As Kosen began cutting up the meat, Matt asked him, "How does the poison work?"

Kosen explained, "The poison makes the animal bleed to death internally, but it doesn't affect the meat at all." He displayed the sharp metal arrowhead with what looked like black gum on it. "I use this type of arrowhead for animals this size," Kosen said. "The head is sharp enough to penetrate the skin and insert the poison, but it usually falls out easily. That way I don't bend the arrowhead and I can use it again. The poison is so strong that if you nick yourself with a poison-tipped arrow you'd be dead within minutes. That's why I wrap it so carefully."

"How do you make the poison?" Matt asked Kosen.

Kosen looked thoughtful. "I can show you how I make the poison, but it is too late now." He indicated the sky. We could see the dull orange of the setting sun against the ragged outline of the volcanic crater in the valley. With a smile he gave us a leg of the bushbuck to take home.

Matt arranged for us to meet Kosen at the tree fort again on Saturday morning and he would show us how he made his poison.

The Dorobo hoisted the rest of the meat and disappeared.

THE POISON ARROW TREE

We chattered like vervet monkeys as we hustled to get home before dark. "Did you see how fast the poison worked? Did you see how silently he walked through the bush? Did any of you see what he was shooting at?" The questions flew back and forth without many answers.

At home I told my dad about the hunting trip and the poison arrow. He listened with interest. And when I told him we'd be going to see how he made the poison on Saturday, he insisted on joining us. I wasn't sure what the other guys would think of my dad tagging along.

I told them the next morning at school. Jon said his dad wanted to come too. As a doctor he was interested in traditional African herbs and medicines and wanted to see how this type of poison was made.

"I really didn't want him to come," Jon said, "but now that your dad is planning on coming too, I guess it won't be so bad."

"We're coming too," Jill said, emerging from behind the big cedar tree where we pounded out the chalkboard erasers. She looked at her friends, Rebekah and Rachel, who nodded.

"You can't leave us out of this adventure," Rebekah said, speaking for her sister who looked a bit embarrassed. The three girls marched off.

Matt snorted and looked disgustedly at me. "This is all your fault, Dean. If you hadn't been so friendly with Jill, they would never have messed up all our fun."

I wanted to protest, but the steely look in Matt's ice-blue eyes stopped me. "I just thought of something," I said, trying to change the subject. "The Dorobo man guaranteed we'd have a genet cat in our trap this morning."

"We'll have to check it right after school this afternoon," Matt said. He paused. "Without the girls!"

When we arrived at the trap we heard a thumping sound. We pulled the trap out and saw a genet cat banging its nose against the mesh-wire screen.

"I can't believe it!" Matt said. "We caught a genet cat."

"Yeah," said Jon. "Look at the beautiful black spots on his back." He wanted to kill it right away.

We didn't have our guns, and I kind of doubted our air guns would kill a genet cat, anyway. "Let's take him home," I suggested. "My dad can take some pictures first."

We took turns carrying the trap home. My dad happily snapped some pictures. We released the genet cat into the small area fenced with chicken wire that we had built to keep our puppies out of trouble. The genet cat darted back and forth inside the wire. My dad couldn't get him to stop long enough to get any decent pictures. The frantic genet cat spotted a small gap under the wire and slid through it and escaped into the woods.

Jon was the only one who was really upset. "I wanted that skin," he said, miffed that the genet cat had gotten away.

Matt consoled him. "We caught one so I'm sure we can catch another one later."

Our attention shifted from genet cat trapping to seeing how the Dorobo made poison.

We tried to sneak away to our tree fort on Saturday morning without the girls following us, but Jill, Rebekah, and Rachel stood under a wild olive tree at the entrance to the forest path waiting for us. We couldn't just tell them to get lost with our dads watching, but Matt's eyes steamed under his khaki safari hat. "Look, Dean," Matt insisted. "We can't show the girls where our tree house is hidden. If they have to go along, why don't I go down first and bring the Dorobo man here before going to make the arrow poison."

I suggested the idea to my dad and he agreed.

"As long as we get to see him making the arrow poison," Jill said.

After half an hour, Matt showed up with the Dorobo hunter.

He and my dad chewed the news for a few minutes. "He says he doesn't live around here," my dad translated. "His family lives about fifty miles away in another forest called Olpusimoru, but he came over here for a few weeks to see what it's like. Farmers are buying up some of the forestland by their home. As they cut down the trees and start planting potatoes and corn, the animals withdraw and it's harder to get all the right trees for the bees to make honey. He's looking around to see if this might be a better place to live."

"What does he think of our forest?" I asked.

"He likes it, but the forested area isn't large enough to support a family for very long. He wants to set up a few beehives. He could harvest them once or twice a year even if he still lives in the

Olpusimoru forest. He says the hunting has been OK, but there are too few animals for more than an occasional hunt."

Jon's dad explained his interest in the poison since he was a doctor. My dad asked if he could take some pictures. Kosen agreed, but he pointed at the girls and frowned and started speaking rapidly while shaking his head.

"What's his problem, Mr. Sandler?" Jill asked.

"I'm sorry, girls, but Kosen has said that girls aren't allowed to see how arrow poison is made. The Dorobo apparently have some very strict rules about making the poison. Kosen says he has to purify himself for several days before making the poison. He can't eat fat, he can't eat salt, he can't use soap, and he can't spend the night with his wife. He's done all those things, but he also says no female is permitted to see how the poison is made. In fact, women or girls aren't even allowed to step over the fireplace where he'll boil the poison."

Rebekah pouted. "I don't believe it! You're just trying to keep us girls out of the adventure."

Dad talked some more with Kosen, who crossed his arms and refused to move. "Sorry, girls," he said. "Kosen is adamant. Girls can't even see the poison on his arrows or it will lose its power. I'm afraid you'll have to head on home. We'll tell you about it later and show you some of the pictures."

"What a rip-off," Jill grumbled as the three girls headed back to Rugendo.

Matt had a smile as wide as the Nile River. After the girls left, Kosen led our parade through the forest.

We hiked downhill until the forest thinned a bit and more sunshine filtered through. Kosen came to a stop beside a stubby tree with branches covered with small green leaves and a few red berries.

He told us this was the tree where he got his poison. Taking his knife, he cut about six branches the width of a fat red cooking banana. He cut them into eight-inch lengths and peeled off the bark and put the shiny-white branches in a battered, smoke-blackened pot. He asked if any of us had brought matches. We hadn't. He shrugged and pulled out a flat piece of cedar and a smooth hand-worn *olpiron* stick that look like a giant pencil. He sent us to collect firewood. Kosen got down on his knees and gathered a small pile of tiny twigs and dried grass. He set the flat piece of wood, about the size of a dollar bill, on the ground. We could see it had a black hole grooved in the center. My dad began focusing and clicking pictures from different angles.

Kosen put the stick into the hole and carefully placed some of his fire-starting twigs and grass around the hole. Taking the stick between the palms of his hands, he began rubbing his hands back and forth, causing the stick to twirl in the hole. Within thirty seconds, his rapid motions had generated heat between the two pieces of wood and some of the straw began to smoke and glow. He stooped over and blew gently on the sparks. Soon the orange glow spread and more of the dried grass and twigs caught fire. Kosen took this start and put it on the ground and started inserting some of the firewood we had brought. Within a few minutes he had a good fire crackling.

He said he needed more firewood and plenty of water to cover the sticks. We scampered around bringing him what he needed. Once the fire had burned into glowing coals, he set his pot of tree bark and water on it and stepped back. He said, "The sticks have to cook for a long time. The water will turn black. The mixture needs to simmer until tomorrow morning. Then there will be a tarlike paste on the bottom. That paste is my arrow poison."

Jon's dad had a lot of questions as to how the poison worked. Kosen explained how it made the animal bleed inside and how it didn't harm the meat. Jon's dad went to the tree and examined the leaves, trying to identify what family of tree it belonged to.

Kosen watched Jon's dad curiously. When Jon's dad started to bend a branch to break it off, the Dorobo quickly told him to stop.

"Why? What's wrong?" Jon's dad asked.

Kosen said, "The tree's poison can be harmful in other ways, and I don't want anyone to be hurt."

"What other ways?" my dad asked. "The berries don't seem to be toxic. The birds are eating them."

"The berries don't seem to bother birds," Kosen said, "but the branches can make a person very sick."

"How?" asked Jon's dad.

"If you cook meat over a fire made of the branches or use the branches as skewers for your meat it can make you very sick. Somehow the poison moves from the smoke or the sticks themselves into the meat. I don't know how it works. We Dorobo are very careful around these trees."

Jon piped up. "I don't know if it means anything, but there's a poison arrow tree right next to the place where Ngugi died."

His dad turned quickly. "There is? Why didn't you tell us before?"

"I didn't know it was a poison arrow tree until this morning when the hunter told us, but I'm sure there's a tree just like this one over by the pond."

"You're right, Jon," I agreed. "That tree is just like this one. Do you think it might be why Ngugi died?"

"I think we should go over there right now and find out," Dr. Freedman said. He and my dad talked with the Dorobo and explained about the two boys getting sick and Ngugi's death. Taking his pot of poison off the fire, Kosen hid it and stamped out the fire, and we headed for the pond.

When we arrived, Jon's dad went straight to the tree and looked closely. "It sure is the same species," he said.

Kosen grunted in agreement. "Yes, this is a poison arrow tree," he said. "I noted its location about a month ago in case I needed it some day for making poison."

I looked at Dave and whispered, "He must have been the shadow we saw the day Ngugi died!" Dave nodded.

Kosen bent over the blackened grass where the boys had cooked their rabbit. Sifting through the remains of the small fire, he picked up some sticks and shook his head sadly. "It looks like the boys cooked their rabbit over branches from the poison arrow tree." He pointed at a sharpened stick. "And one of the boys used a green branch to spear his meat and hold it over the fire. I'm sure that's why the one boy died."

"Poisoned by the poison arrow tree," my dad mused. "Now this puts a different light on these spiritual attacks that are continuing against Kamau's family. We'd better go over and talk to them right away."

"Wait a minute," Dr. Freedman said. "What about all that spiritual warfare stuff when Kamau got sick the second time and he and Jon almost died? Was that also caused by the poison arrow tree?"

"No," my dad said. "That was definitely a spiritual attack brought on by the witch doctor. We Christians weren't prepared and some of our mean-spirited gossiping and unresolved anger that we try to excuse as frustration over cultures clashing had actually given Satan a foothold and left us open to attack. What this means, though, is that Ngugi's death was not caused by any spiritual forces. It didn't happen—as the witch doctor and Ngugi's father maintain—because Kamau's family annoyed the ancestral spirits. Ngugi was poisoned after cooking his meat on a stick from this tree. If we can explain that to Kamau's family and then go and share this with Ngugi's family, we should be able to stop Ngugi's father from invoking any more calamities on Kamau's family."

My dad felt it was important to resolve things between the two families as soon as possible. "Let's go find Pastor Waweru and some of the church elders," he said to Dr. Freedman. "We'll take Kosen with us to explain about the poison arrow tree."

"Can we come?" I asked. Dad looked uncertain.

"Please," I begged. "Kamau has become our friend. We want to see the end of all these curses on his family."

Dad nodded. "All right, you can come along."

We went to Kamau's family first. After greeting everyone, my dad asked, "Kamau, when you and Ngugi roasted that rabbit, where did you get the firewood?"

"We used sticks from under a nearby tree," Kamau answered.

"And what kind of sticks did you use for roasting the meet?" my dad went on.

"Ngugi used a green branch from that same tree as his cooking stick. I cut a stick from a green wattle tree nearby," Kamau said.

"That explains why Ngugi died and Kamau survived," Dr.

Freedman stated. He had stopped and done a bit of research from a botany book while we waited for Pastor Waweru to gather some of the church elders. "According to the books, this tree, which our Dorobo friend Kosen calls the poison arrow tree, produces an anti-coagulant poison that is undetectable."

"What's that anti-whatever he said?" I whispered to Matt.

He shrugged.

Kamau and his parents looked puzzled, too.

Dr. Freedman explained, "Anticoagulant means the poison stops the blood from clotting so the victim bleeds to death internally very quickly. It's just like Kosen said. The poison is untraceable. That's why the lab could find nothing when the boys were sick. And even the bones you Rhinos found by their fire showed no trace of poison."

"If this is true," Kamau's father said, "we must go tell Ngugi's father at once."

"Are you ready to forgive Ngugi's father?" Pastor Waweru asked.

"Forgive him? Why should I forgive him?" Kamau's father asked, his voice trembling. "He called down a sickness that almost killed Kamau. Now he's killed one of my cows. I want him to stop, but I don't want to forgive him!"

"Unless you're willing to confess your bitterness and anger over being attacked, you can't forgive Ngugi's father," Pastor Waweru explained. "And if you hold onto unforgiveness and bitterness, your family will still be open to spiritual attack."

Baba Kamau's crossed his arms and stared at Pastor Waweru. Kamau looked at his father and then at Pastor Waweru. He looked back at his father, but the man hadn't moved. Kamau bent his head and studied the ground intently. At last he knelt down.

"Father God, forgive me for being angry with Ngugi's father," he prayed loudly enough for everyone to hear. His own father glared. A moment later Kamau's mother fell to her knees and cried out for forgiveness. She put her arm around Kamau.

The hardness in Kamau's father's eyes faded and they glistened with tears. He turned to Pastor Waweru. "I must also confess my anger. Will you pray with me?" Pastor Waweru knelt down and prayed with the family. When they finished, Kamau's father stood up and brushed the dirt from the knees of his trousers.

"If you're ready to forgive Ngugi's father, we can go and explain to them about the poison arrow tree," Pastor Waweru said.

Kamau's father nodded. "God has forgiven me. I must forgive others."

We went as a team to Ngugi's family. My dad told them how the poison arrow tree had caused of Ngugi's death. Ngugi's father glared at us. He said, "I don't know if I believe your story."

Kosen explained clearly about the poison. Ngugi's father listened intently, but then hissed, "Someone must still pay for Ngugi's death!"

Kamau stepped forward and said, "I forgive you for making me sick and for killing our cow." Kamau's parents followed, confessing their own anger and forgiving Ngugi's father for the curses he had invoked on their family.

The spirit of forgiveness really rocked Ngugi's father. Dr. Freedman, tears in his eyes, also confessed that he had been angry at Ngugi's father because of the curse on Jon. "God, I ask you to forgive me for my anger," Dr. Freedman prayed out loud. He looked at Ngugi's father. "And I ask you to forgive me for my angry thoughts against you."

Ngugi's father trembled. "How can you forgive me after what I've done?" he asked. Ngugi's father slumped onto a wooden chair outside his house and asked Pastor Waweru to stay and tell him more about Jesus. "There's something here too powerful for me to understand. How can Kamau and his family forgive me?"

On the way home, Kosen said to my dad, "Your Jesus seems powerful. Can you come visit our village and tell us the words about God?"

"I'd love to come to your village," Dad answered. They arranged a time and place so Kosen could guide my dad to their forest home.

Back at Rugendo, we walked toward Matt's house. "I need a snack," Matt announced. "My mom said she was going to bake cookies."

We walked into a comforting blanket of warm cookie aroma at Matt's house. Matt pulled some cold Cokes from the fridge.

"Looks like we got to the bottom of the mystery," Matt said as we drank Cokes and ate peanut butter cookies on the veranda of his house.

"Yeah, a poison arrow tree," said Jon. "I wonder if we could brew up our own pot of poison? The recipe didn't look that hard."

"No way," said Dave. "That stuff is scary. It can kill. I'm not sure I want to eat pigeons any more. What if they'd been eating the berries?"

We laughed. "It's potent poison," Matt said, "but not that dangerous, Dave. Besides, for some reason it doesn't affect birds. That's another mystery."

"Well, I'm definitely not going to try to solve that mystery," Dave said firmly.

Just then Jill walked by with Rachel and Rebekah. "So you've given up on solving the mystery?" Jill asked. "We girls would never give up, even if that man wouldn't let us watch him make arrow poison."

"Oh, we did solve the mystery of how Ngugi died," Matt said, boasting like a bullfrog. "Dave's talking about why birds don't get harmed by eating berries from the poison arrow tree. Ngugi was poisoned by the poison arrow tree."

"That's not fair," said Jill after we'd explained the whole story. "You didn't solve the mystery. The Dorobo hunter did. If there's ever another mystery to solve around here, we'll find the answers first." The girls flounced out, whispering to each other.

"Not if we can help it," Matt shouted after them. He bit into another cookie and smiled. "The Rhinos are the best!"